KILLEBRITY

James Nowlan

copyright 2015
ISBN 978-2-9554655-0-9

ONE

Mike Johnson was hot and uncomfortable in his new blazer and slacks, and he had never liked wearing a tie. It reminded him of being on the parade ground for dress review, an event that had always been a moment of anxiety for him. He disliked the idea of being inspected and possibly criticized. Getting out in the field had been a relief. Sure, a person could get horribly wounded or even killed at any moment, but there were never any disparaging words accompanying the injury.

Now he was going to an interview for a job he didn't really want, dressed in clothes he couldn't afford to buy, and in a neighborhood where everyone was so filthy, unkempt, and drunk, or high on drugs that they seemed to be there specifically to deride his relatively clean cut and sober appearance. Walking anywhere in Los Angeles always makes a person feel like a non-entity, but the stretch that he had made from the bus stop to the low rent office where he had his appointment had reduced him to a state where he felt like a ghost, floating along through the walking dead who staggered down the sidewalks panhandling or collecting cans to pay for their next bottle or high.

The most disturbing part of it was that he had almost fallen as low as them. After getting back from overseas he had been on a two week long drunk which was for the most part a black hole. He had stopped because he was afraid of what he was turning into. As he became progressively sloppier and more belligerent he realized that he was doing and saying things that were going to get him in trouble (even though most of what had happened during his binges was a mystery).

He hated the conversations he could remember having with people. They always started with, "So what are you doing in LA?" He didn't feel like explaining. He'd been moving around since before he could remember. His mother, after getting fed up with her lousy job and crummy apartment, picked up and moved on to what was often even drearier shelter and employment. She'd always stayed in Los Angeles County for some reason. Mike had thought about it once and wondered if it wasn't some sort of court order or maybe a superstition.

Anyway it left Mike with a conundrum. He was from LA but he wasn't from any particular part of LA. If he told locals it was his home they'd accuse him of trying to pose as an Angeleno when he wasn't, and if he went anywhere else in America he'd be looked upon as a freak. California, and especially Los Angeles, were places one went to, not away from; its natives were viewed as strange birds who couldn't flourish in less exotic climes.

So there he was, no place to call home. He had no explanation for himself. He'd thought the military would give him a sense of belonging but fighting in a foreign country had left him feeling more rootless than ever. So he had prowled from bar to bar getting into increasingly uglier confrontations with people until he awoke one morning on the floor of his low rent motel room with particularly bad recollections lurking in his mind.

He vaguely remembered being in a seventies themed singles bar. There were posters of stars like Farah Fawcett, Erik Estrada, and John Travolta on the walls. Multi-color disco lights flashed and swirled while ABBA played. The gaudily dressed clientele shook their booties in homage to the most superficial decade of the twentieth century. But Mike, impervious to the garish scene, sat perched on a stool, mesmerized by a television report about Al Qaida that was playing on the big screen behind the bar. The sound was almost entirely drowned out by the clamor of some sorority girls standing next to him. What he heard was, "oh my god! TERROR, la dee da, TERROR, you let him do that! TERROR." Then Osama Bin Laden's face appeared on the screen. He studied the face of Bin Laden, the smile smug and serene, rather like that of Mona Lisa. The image of the bearded terrorist seemed to grow and glow until it filled the room taking possession of him. He jumped up on the bar screaming "Allah

Akbar", and began making shooting movements with his hands.

He had no idea how he had gotten home. He felt himself all over to see if he'd broken anything while intoxicated. Apart from a few bruises, probably gotten by falling on the stairs, he was uninjured, but his wallet was gone. He turned his pockets inside out and found nothing but a business card. He threw the card on the night table and began frantically searching for the holder of his ID, money, and credit cards. He found it inexplicably stuck under his shirt and shoes near the door.

After he had calmed down he picked up the card. It was for a security agency, "Hollywood Detectives". On the back was written, "I think this might be the right place for you, at least until you get back on your feet." For signature there was nothing but an extravagantly etched K. He'd no idea who "K" was or how his card had gotten into his pocket.

He reread the words on the back. Amidst all the hostility, someone out there had felt a moment of pity for him. He gripped the card with the index and forefinger of both hands and held it close to his eyes, searching for the reason that it was in his pocket. Finding none he decided to look further.

The storefront internet cafe across the street was awfully sleazy, one could almost smell the scent of porn rising from the cubicles. Behind the counter there was a perky girl in large glasses and a t-shirt with the name of some obscure indy band. Disturbingly, she seemed to know him. He wondered if something might have happened between them during a drunken blackout.

She asked him if he wanted a headset. When he declined she protested. "But how are you going to talk and hear?" He shook his head and went to the place whose number she had given him. He googled "Hollywood Detectives" and visited its website.

He clicked onto its recruitment page. It showed several shots of men in black bomber jackets holding back frenzied packs of fans that were mobbing celebrities. It didn't really look like where he wanted to be, but he had to be somewhere. Then he read the caption "Be A Star of Security", and an idea formed in his head.

He would tell them he was an aspiring actor and wanted to get into show business, even though nothing could be further from the truth. He'd taken some acting and film courses during the semester he'd spent in college classrooms trying to complete a distance learning degree. It'd been such a depressing experience that it ultimately led him to drop out and thoroughly disgusted him with the idea of having anything to do with the motion picture industry. Even now the thought of pretending to be a wannabe movie extra was distasteful to him. But he would have explanations, a reason for why he was in LA, and an excuse for why he didn't apply to a law enforcement agency.

"I, just like everybody else, want to be a star," he'd tell them and by claiming this similitude he would become something like what everybody else was. So he sent an email with his resume attached and was surprised when he got a positive response a few hours later, a job interview not far from where he was staying.

When he got to the shabby mini-mall whose address he had been given he asked himself if he was at the right place. Apart from the gleaming entrance of a convenience store that provided the junk food that the neighborhood's derelicts used to supplement their diet of drugs and alcohol, every storefront seemed to be boarded up or burnt out.

He was wondering if he had gotten the directions wrong when he caught sight of a corrugated metal structure at the end of the parking lot. Approaching it he noticed the name of the company that he was applying for a position with written in red letters on a black metal plaque, "Hollywood Detectives". A doorbell button was positioned right next to it but something made him hesitate. The name "Hollywood Detectives" conjured up some unpleasant feelings. It evoked the glamorous and the sordid as well as the sublime and the subterranean. The very colors it was printed in conveyed a sort of menace, red and black, drops of blood in the night. But at night blood isn't red but shades of gray like everything else (or a phosphorescent green if you happened to be looking through night vision goggles). He seemed to be looking through some strange sort of lenses himself now, everything around him flattened and unreal in spite of the chaos and decay, a sound stage meticulously set up to represent urban deterioration at its worst, and he the lead player having forgotten his lines.

He pushed the button and a bell rang so loudly that he jumped back in fright. He waited for several uncomfortable minutes, not daring to set off the bell that sounded more like a distress signal than a door buzzer. He had just about gotten up the nerve to ring it again when a voice, rendered almost inaudible by the static of a short circuiting speaker, came over the intercom, "Hey, you. Look up here." He looked up into the lens of a surveillance camera that pivoted towards him, the iris inside expanding suddenly like that of a person who had just died or been injected with a powerful drug.

The voice crackled louder, "So, you're the new guy. I recognize you from your picture."

"Yeah, it's me, Mike Johnson, we talked on the phone yesterday."

"Okay, I'll let you in." With a noise like the buzzing of an angry insect the steel reinforced door unlocked and Mike stepped into a hallway filled with air that had been cooled and disinfected, a welcome relief from the hot putrid gases outside. He walked down the passage trying not to be affected by the pictures along the wall. They were a curious combination of celebrity portraits and crime scene photos. In one frame would be a famous face smiling congenially and in the following a body that had suffered a brutal death.

At the end of the hallway he arrived at an office whose walls were lined with files reaching to the ceiling. Seated behind a desk that used up most of the available space, a man was working at a portable computer. He looked up for an instant revealing a haggard sunburned face whose gray eyes scanned the job applicant like those of an aging cowboy watching a wayward calf that was wandering about at the limit of the horizon.

The man looked back down at his computer screen and the expression on his face changed from inquisitional to slightly perplexed. "I've just got to finish something I'm working on here. Do you know how to spell the word 'impostor'? Someone who's pretending to be something he's not?"

Without too much reflection Mike sounded out, "I,M,P,O,S,T,O,R."

"Damn I guess you've read a book or two. Are you sure it's not I,M,P,O,S,T,U,R,E?"

Mike responded quickly and assuredly, "No that's the act of pretending to be something you're not itself."

For several uncomfortable seconds Mike was forced to endure the probing stare of his potential employer. "You must have studied hard." The man rose from his seat with a peculiar sort of grace, a bit like a time lapse film of flowers rising towards the sun, and reached towards Mike as if his arm was a growing branch with the hand at the end of it a bud opening. Mike took the hand and shook it and felt the grip itself as a sort of interrogation; somehow some deep knowledge was being sucked out of him by the man before him. "I'm Moses Murphy," said the possessor of the invasive palm and fingers, "have a seat." He let go of Mike's hand with a flourish like that of a magician performing a trick and waved towards an uncomfortable looking rusty folding chair squeezed amongst the stacks of files.

Mike made a place for himself, as well as he could, and then looked up again into Moses' challenging gaze. "So security, not really high up on the list of career choices," Moses stated discouragingly. "Why is a clever, clean cut boy like you looking for a job with us?"

"Well," Mike replied with a slightly self-conscious voice, "When I was in Iraq and Afghanistan they sometimes showed us war movies, and watching them I wondered why some guy should make millions for pretending to be what I really was. I felt that if I could just get my moment on screen I'd be a star. I thought that a job like this might help make the contacts I might need to get that moment."

"First you went to war, then you came to Hollywood? You think you're going to meet some people who will hook you up? Damn, how many times have I heard that? Do you think that these people really want to know you?" Mike squirmed in his seat as much as the limited space would allow. "I guess we all need to keep hold of our dreams no matter how pathetic they might be. Have you ever thought of giving up the booty? Maybe the right sugar daddy will make those dreams come true."

Mike's face flushed red with anger and he seemed to inflate, his entire body pushing back against his narrow confines. "Ha, ha, ha," Moses laughed, "Hey, you got to keep a sense of humor about it. Hell, anything might happen. You might just save somebody's life. Or you could catch them doing something really bad. I think the second one is better. Gratitude doesn't go so far with a lot of people but when you have the dirt on them then they're your bitch and you can treat them how you want. Why you think I got all this?" He raised his hands indicating the boxes of files filling the room which, through Moses' simple gesture, were transformed from musty smelling paper into a powerful mystery. "I know everything about everyone, that's how I stay in business. It's not just a matter of knowing that they're crazy; it's knowing what kind of crazy they are. You're not crazy are you?"

Mike hesitated, asking himself if this man could know. The agreement he had made. How he had stood before a grim panel of examiners and it had been decided. He wouldn't seek any sort of disability benefits, and they would bury the file that lay there on the desk before them. He'd get a normal discharge and he could live free of the label "mentally disturbed" that would follow him around otherwise. Posttraumatic stress disorder, that's the conclusion most of the doctors had reached. Others simply labeled him psychotic for convenience's sake, that way they could claim his state arose from a pre-existing condition and was therefore not something that would qualify him for a military pension. What's more, if Mike had psychosis on his discharge papers then he would probably never find a job, even in fast food. The manager would be afraid, no matter how timid Mike might seem, that someday he would come to work with an automatic rifle and the clients would get a side of .223 Remington along with their burger and fries.

Moses simply eyed him impassively. No, he couldn't know Mike's medical history, if he had known he would never have asked him in for this interview. So Mike forced the feeling that was rising within him back down. He tried to erase from his mind the ugly memories that would betray him with a twitch or a shudder if he let them, and he answered with an empty look on his face and a flat voice, "Absolutely not, I'm perfectly sane, you have my file don't you."

"Of course I have your file, I wouldn't hire you without it," Moses stated dismissively. "But one can never know. The objective of this agency is to protect stars from the crazies, so I can't be hiring crazies myself can I. Well actually, I once did hire a serious nut job just as a sort of experiment. He thought he was bullet proof because of some ninja powers he had acquired. It would have been fine. He would work anytime anywhere and do everything exactly as asked, but in the end a problem developed. He couldn't stop from sharing his craziness with the world, and he'd tell the clients about the 'powers' that he had, that he could read the minds of evildoers and other sorts of insanity. So one day I called him in here and he sat where you're sitting right now and I opened this drawer," Moses slid the top drawer of his desk out, "I got out this gun," he pulled out a .32 caliber colt revolver, "I pointed it at him," Moses pointed the gun at Mike, "and I pulled the trigger." Moses pulled the trigger and before the report of the gun even rang out Mike was scrambling for cover in the stacks of files, frantically trying to dig as deeply as possible away from the bullets that he imagined already hitting him, causing a shock that rendered him impervious to pain.

He stopped when he heard Moses laughing behind him. "It's loaded with blanks, of course neither you nor he could know this. He reacted in a way more extreme than yourself. He started screaming something in some strange language and then fell comatose to the floor. We had to call an ambulance to cart him off to the hospital. Anyway it looks like you'll do just fine. I kind of need a personal assistant right now and you seem right for the job."

So Moses laid a contract out in front of Mike and with a trembling hand he started to fill it out. Filling out forms and signing contracts was another thing that made Mike nervous. How could one know what they were really getting into? You'd have to be a lawyer and even lawyers would give you contradictory advice. But the whole idea of writing down his work and education history was even more anxiety inducing. He felt that he was perpetuating a lie that almost anyone could see through. He was supposedly in a certain place at a certain time doing certain things. But at the time he had felt like a fraud who was just going through the motions and, even though he had in fact accomplished the tasks he was assigned, he just didn't feel that it had been done by him but by some kind of force external to himself pushing him to do it, as if he were a marionette or a remote controlled robot. But he needed this job, both for the money and to stop ruminating over the past, so once again he forced himself to hide his true feelings and keep the emotions churning inside from making his face into a spastic jellyfish.

When he had finished Moses casually appraised it while pinching its corners with his fingertips and then filed it away. "Well, that's that, you're officially part of the team. Feel any different?" Mike shrugged his shoulders. "Yeah," Moses continued, "you don't seem to me like someone who has a need to belong. Some people will do anything in order not to feel unwanted. Like this crazy guy I talked to you about before. After he got out of the psych ward he wouldn't give his uniform back. He kept showing up at different sites telling people he was working there that day. We had to keep finding a means to coax him away. Eventually we convinced him to get on disability and take medication. I hear he goes to group therapy sessions dressed up like a security guard; he even wears a baseball cap with 'SECURITY' printed on it."

"I find that hard to imagine," Mike said, "Not to denigrate your work here, but it's not like you're part of some elite military group or something, is it? You don't have a special tattoo or anything do you?"

"A tattoo," muttered Moses speculatively, "Maybe that's just what we need, but what could it be?"

"Maybe a vulture feasting on some carrion in the middle of the desert," Mike suggested.

"That would be too close to the truth," Moses said, "and if there is one thing we want to avoid it's the truth. You can tell one story or another to make this or that group or individual happy, but if you tell the truth you're going to have everyone angry at you."

"I guess you're right, all my worst troubles have come from being too truthful."

"If you've gotten to that point of seeing things then you've got what it takes to do this job. Let's take a ride so I can give you an understanding of the territory you'll be working."

"I already know the neighborhood pretty well."

"I'm not talking about just knowing it but about acquiring a certain feeling of it."

"Alright," Mike replied quizzically, "whatever you say."

TWO

Moses led Mike down the corridor without a glance at the pictures on the wall and stepped out into the stagnant heat of the parking lot. He had started walking towards a white Ford LTD when he noticed a grime coated street person sitting on the hood, incongruously shivering in the sweltering sun. "Hey, you, who the hell's car you think you're sitting on?"

"Oh, I didn't know," stuttered the derelict.

"You must have known that it belonged to someone and that that someone wouldn't be too happy about you lounging on top of their ride."

"Oh, I'm sorry, I should have thought of that," he slurred and he rolled off the hood.

"At least you're starting to think, damn, why don't you get on SSI and section eight housing, that way you could be indoors watching reruns of Star

Trek or whatever instead of being a public nuisance."

"I'm trying," whined the homeless man, "but they put me on a waiting list."

"A waiting list for what? SSI or section eight housing?" queried Moses.

"Both."

"Both? I don't think so. You look disturbed enough to get SSI right away-how long you'll have to wait for a section eight apartment is another matter."

"Um, they told me to apply when I got released from the state hospital, but I don't know what's happening with my case now."

"State hospital huh? People there should have fixed things up before letting you loose."

"I had trouble communicating with them."

"Hey, you're going to have to learn how to if you don't want to get into trouble. What are you doing in the meantime?"

"Just waiting."

"Well here," Moses plucked five dollars out of his wallet, "have yourself a drink, but don't buy anything cheap because it makes you puke your guts out, and it's bad for my business to have vomit all over my parking lot. Get yourself some merlot, or chardonnay, or something like that."

"Okay," the street person mumbled obsequiously, and his trembling diminished in anticipation of the calming effects of a good bottle of wine. Moses observed him detachedly as if studying a laboratory animal. He then opened the door of his LTD and swung into its broiling hot interior.

"Damn, if there is one thing I'm going to do when I get some money it's to get some covered parking so I can leave my ride in the shade."

Mike winced from the heat. "Yeah, but that might encourage street people to make this place their home; they'd have a roof over their heads."

Moses started the motor and switched on the air conditioning that at first did nothing but recycle the hot air, blasting it into their faces like a machine meant to scald the surfacing off of something. "Yeah, well there are all degrees of street people: some of them harmlessly insane like that guy I gave a fiver too, others aggressive drunks, and even a few criminals who are so bad at crime or so addicted to drugs that they can't get enough money together to pay for a hotel room. I deal with all of them differently, not because I'm a particularly nice guy, but because they're all different kinds of problems that call for different solutions. We're going to cruise around a bit and maybe meet some other troublesome individuals so you can see how I handle them."

The air conditioning kicked in and a Freon cooled breeze washed over Mike. Moses pointed at the glove compartment, "There's something in there for you."

Mike opened the glove compartment and found a thirty two caliber Colt revolver like the one that had been fired at him earlier. "Is that all I rate?" he objected, "a thirty two?"

Moses settled back in the leather seating that in the sweltering heat had been cloyingly sticky but was now becoming comfortable. "I start everybody off with that piece. There's nothing wrong with it. It's the gun that Charles Bronson used in Death Wish."

Mike flicked the cylinder open. "It's not even loaded."

"There's also a box of cartridges."

Mike began loading the gun.

Reaching over Moses pulled a box of blank cartridges out as well. "Here put one of these in the first chamber."

"What the hell?"

"Hey, that's my standard procedure. Until I know how you act under pressure I want your first shot to just scare people instead of wounding them."

"Damn."

"But that's the breaks. I'm the one who's going to have to go to all the trouble of getting you a concealed carry permit, and if you accidentally shoot someone that's going make life a lot harder for me."

Mike sighed in resignation and, after putting a blank in the first chamber and live rounds in the rest, started to stick the revolver in his belt.

Moses shook his head disapprovingly, "There's a holster in there too. It's safer. Just sticking your pistol in your crotch could do some serious damage to your equipment. Didn't they teach you how to carry a handgun when you were in Iraq and Afghanistan?"

"Well, normally we weren't issued small arms."

"Oh yeah?"

"But I procured a twenty two caliber automatic and concealed it in an ankle holster."

"What good was that supposed to do you on the battlefield?"

"Make sure I wasn't taken alive."

"Damn, I can understand that. Just keep that thirty two in the holster on your belt and you won't be taken alive by any of the hostiles here either."

Mike complied and Moses eased the car out of the parking lot and into traffic. They cruised the streets of Hollywood for a while, and Mike gazed out at the passing scenery. It was transformed completely by his vantage point of being inside a large air-conditioned car, the subtropical flora and eclectic architecture that had made him feel disoriented when he had strolled through it as a pedestrian became a fascinating spectacle that he felt well insulated from. It was a bit like a ride in Disneyland, being on a safari in a four wheel drive truck, or even exploring another planet in a space rover. He almost felt that he should congratulate whoever had put together these baroque tableaus that now unfolded before his eyes.

Moses broke this spell, "You see here what we have is a sort of frontier between two groups that need to be kept apart, I guess you know how that works." Mike nodded. "The people there on top," he pointed toward the distant Hollywood Hills barely visible through a haze of car exhaust, "got more power than they know what do with and whatever kind of mistakes they make stand very little chance of being punished no matter how badly they fuck up." He then squinted his eyes as if to protect them from some toxic spray, "But the people here are totally powerless and can be hauled off to jail for jaywalking." Mike took in the surroundings with a comprehending look on his face. "Where we come into the equation is when these two worlds meet. The people on top coming into contact with the people on the bottom, usually for drugs or sex or something like that."

"Sounds like we're rangers in a wildlife preserve or something."

"That's about it. The place we're going to visit now has been taking care of one of our clients."

"Oh, yeah what's wrong with them?"

"The usual: drugs, alcohol, insanity, sexual perversion. She's a fine example of how this jungle can mess an individual up. Her mother was some white trash bitch who came here to pimp her out to all the freaks with connections in this town when she was about thirteen years old. She kept her daughter quiet about all the sick things that were being done to her underage booty with a combination of heavy medication and some kind of voodoo mind control doled out by a sleaze with a license to practice psychotherapy."

Mike screwed up his face in disgust, "But couldn't something be done? Wouldn't somebody step in to prevent that from happening?"

"Welcome to the real world Dorothy," Moses intoned gravely. "Nobody cares. That's the way things work here. She eventually got hooked up with some scumbag producer who got her a role in a TV show for kids. So then you've got the drugged out teenage sex toy of Hollywood presented as a squeaky clean model for America's adolescent girls and helping mess up their minds too. She goes on to sing some sappy songs about being a confused horny slut, and all the mixed up young females in the heartland buy copies of it. Now she's a media asset and we've got to protect her not just from her fans, but from herself as well because she's one self-destructive little teen idol."

They cruised silently for a while and Mike was almost lulled to sleep by the cool air wafting over him, the luxurious leather seat, and the floating movement of the large Ford as it drifted through traffic. He would perhaps have slept but for troubling memories that kept him awake, memories of other rides that had started calmly and ended in fire and blood. He remembered half instinctively that the worse ambushes almost always came down when everything seemed pacific. His partially closed eyes darted back and forth and his cheeks quivered like someone having a nightmare. Moses glanced over at him. "Don't be going to sleep now, we're going to make contact."

Mike sat up with a start, "Where? What's that?"

"No need to get excited, I'm going to handle it."

"Handle what?"

"Don't worry, just stay in the car and watch."

Moses pulled the LTD to the curb in front of a building that looked like a hospital but was surrounded by a wall like that of a medium security correctional facility. A group of sordid looking characters on the sidewalk lawn in front seemed to be playing some unusual game of catch with unseen people inside, leaping to snatch out of the air small packages that were thrown over the wall and sticking them in the waist bands of their underwear before taking out other packages and throwing them back. When Moses rolled the heavy car up onto the curb all but two of them shambled off, trying to make it look like it was their own idea and that they weren't in any way intimidated.

The remaining pair waited with an insouciance that defied the heat. One was dressed in a worn bronco buster outfit, jeans, plaid shirt, western boots and a Stetson. The other had on some sort of biker get up but without the patches of any motorcycle club. They were obviously the most pathetic sort of poseurs. They hadn't been able to make it as real cowboys or bikers so now they were peddling drugs to junkies in rehab.

Moses put the handbrake on with a slow and deliberate gesture. Its ratcheting sound recalled that of some archaic weapon being armed. He undid his seat belt, opened the door, and slipped out of the car with one seamless stealthy movement, never taking his eyes off the failed gangsters on the lawn. As they recognized him a momentary loss of stoicism flitted across their faces, but they managed to master it and regain their habitual hardened expressions. It was too late however, Moses had caught a glimpse of their discomfiture and he smiled already in triumph. He knew that the two would feel obliged to play out their tough guy scenario, but he knew also that he would make them crumble.

To open this short piece of theater played for a limited audience, Moses mopped his face with a handkerchief. He strolled up to them with the graceful nonchalance of a matador. Back when he was on the police force he had gone south of the border to watch some bullfights on the recommendation of a Mexican colleague. At first he hadn't much understood it, and he probably never understood it as a Mexican or a Spaniard would, but for some reason he became possessed by a need to understand. He went on vacation to Spain and even the south of France, where he watched bulls matched against women matadors on horseback. Gradually a certain feeling for the event grew within him. The feeling expanded till it became more insightful than understanding ever could be. This is the world and this is life, a bloody struggle. Most people would rather hide from this truth but Moses embraced it. The bull is there. The bull is always there, ready to gore you and toss you in the air like a sack of flesh and bones. The thing is to play the bull. Come as close as you can to its horns, all the time preserving the appearance of cool stately grace.

Of course the men he was now preparing to confront had come to a similar conclusion in the course of their lives filled with violence. But they would probably not be able to articulate it very well and would never really find a way to use this knowledge in any sort of productive way, and thus they were relegated to a life of petty criminality.

Still, they felt a need to exude a certain verve, so they cocked their heads at a disjointed angle, a bit like a fighting rooster about to be thrown into the pen, and waited for Moses to make the first move. He looked down and pointed to their feet. They were standing just inside the green border of the lawn. "You gentlemen are on private property," he scolded a bit schoolmarmishly. They choked back an impulse to apologize and moved the conversation up a notch.

The cowboy spoke first, "Hell, whosever property this might be it ain't yours so it ain't any of your business."

Then the biker decided to chime in, "Hey, this is that chump that left the police to start some kind of security service to protect rich people." He then scrutinized Moses for a while, "Yeah, I know him, he's called Moses. Hey, you gonna lead your people to the promisedland? But then where the hell are your people? You're not with the force no more so you don't got no people." He paused to nod his head disdainfully at Mike, "Except for that goofy looking kid in the car, and he don't look like he's worth too much."

"I guess I'm just all alone in this world," Moses murmured reflexively.

"Yeah, you're nothing but a security guard with pretensions of having some kind of game; damn rent a cop, run along and serve your masters," retorted the man in black leather and denim.

"Some kind of game huh?" Moses caressed his chin as if contemplatively stroking a beard that wasn't there. "Yeah I guess some could think of it that way, but a game has rules doesn't it? Who's making the rules for the game we're playing?"

"I've got my own little rule maker right here," the drug dealer retorted, opening his vest to reveal a tiny automatic, "and it says you're out. You're not the police so we don't gotta be afraid of you."

Moses stared down as if fascinated by the tiny weapon in the criminal's sweaty waist band. He pointed a finger at it. "Are those little things coming back in style? How do you keep it in place? Doesn't it move around a lot? How do you keep from accidently shooting yourself with it?"

Moses continued to point his finger at the weapon, his wrist and forearm at a strange angle, like an infant who hasn't yet learned to control its muscles or a person suffering from a neurodegenerative illness. His face also took on an expression of someone in a semi-vegetative state. The two petty dope peddlers didn't know how to respond to this sudden transformation of their adversary. Should they shoot him? His appearance was so pathetic that killing him would be almost like murdering a crippled child.

But as they pondered upon what course of action to take they failed to remark that all this time Moses was getting nearer, his approach seemingly no more of a threat than that of a lamb in a petting zoo, and, shielded by their inattention, he sidled into range. His attack was accompanied by such a sudden change in character that it caught them flatfooted. He was helped not only by his lengthy study of bullfights but a couple of years spent in the ring when he was a teenager.

He had learnt there that boxing could be more efficacious than what certain "experts" expounded as "deadly" martial arts. You just had to learn the basics, distance, guard, footwork, and of course the left jab. His boxing coach had endlessly emphasized the importance of the left jab. But most of the kids training with him had paid little mind, simply throwing themselves at their opponent and flailing away. Moses, however, trained his jab. At first it was of little service and he received many beatings, but when he had perfected it the other kids couldn't get close to him.

And now, decades later, he had maneuvered himself into to a position where he could make use of this well-honed weapon. His left hand shot out from his chin, the limp fingers consolidating into a solid fist in mid-air and landing upon the gun toting dealer's nose, fracturing bone and splitting cartilage. As the left snapped back the right sprang forward and snatched the pistol from its bearer's vest, so fluidly that from his perspective it came off as a skillful sleight of hand. One moment he was gawking at Moses' imbecilic pantomime and the next instant the blank face had filled with fury and was glaring at him over the sights of his own gun.

"Yeah," chuckled Moses, "how the fuck did that happen? I mean like, you're supposed to be so dangerous and everything." The cowboy lunged at Moses but was stopped by a quick kick to his knee and the butt of the gun being brought down on his temple. The two of them were now on all fours bleeding. "Damn that must have been some real exceptional sort of accident. How did you come to be with your heads in the grass like grazing sheep, and me standing over you like a shepherd come to lead you back to the flock?" The crumpled outlaw who had been so craftily disarmed raised his middle finger to Moses, who took as good of a bead on it as he could down the slide of the cheap pistol. "You know I would just blow that off and do you a favor but this is a hospital here and so," he reduced his voice almost to a whisper, "sound must be kept to a minimum." He administered several savage kicks to the midsections of each of them. The blows were accompanied by the sickening sounds of tissue and bones being ruptured and broken. The flamboyantly dressed duo groaned in pain. "Sssssh," Moses hissed, putting a finger to his lips, "quiet."

Moses stood surveying the damage he had done. "Jesus Christ, I guess I done fucked up now. I mean if I was still working for the police department I'd probably get severely sanctioned. But wait I'm not with the department so what does that mean. Hmm, I'll just tell the patrol officers for this division (who by the way happen to be part time employees of mine when they're off duty) that two drug dealing scumbags got high and were savagely beaten by a rogue ex-police officer turned rent a thug to the stars. Seeing that you're both multiple felons who can get a third strike for narcotics possession you might just get life as habitual offenders. Hmm, maybe you can just go to the emergency room, say that you were attacked from behind, and you never got a good look at who it was."

Moses started backing away towards his car. It didn't seem as though he felt too threatened to turn his back on them but rather that he was enjoying the spectacle of their suffering. He caught hold of the door handle and slipped in behind the wheel. The pair, who just a short while before had been carrying on a relatively carefree and highly profitable enterprise, now lay agonizing on the grass. Moses felt this situation shouldn't be wasted but put to an educative purpose. "You see that's the thing; they never expected it to end this way. They thought they were more in control than they really were. You always got to have that end game in sight and be maneuvering towards it. They should have known that as soon as they hit the streets in their super villain suits they'd be obliged to deal with someone who wasn't just playing dress up."

Mike sat silently for several long seconds as if stunned by the events he'd just witnessed, but actually, even more extreme sequences were playing in his mind, scenes too disturbing for the general audience and so cut out. "You know if we did that to a civilian and got caught we'd be in serious trouble."

"Damn they're not civilians they're drug dealers, and I don't give them any points for being amateur clown drug dealers." Moses looked down at the ugly little firearm in his palm. "I guess I'll just add this to my collection," he mumbled before driving off.

THREE

When the car had vanished over the horizon and it seemed like there was no chance of it coming back the drug dealers crept out of their hiding places, but the throwing of packages did not recommence. It was as if they were naughty children who had been so harshly scolded by a cantankerous adult for playing in the street that it had lost all its fun.

Meanwhile in the supposed sanctuary from illicit substances, the barriers holding the storms of intoxication at bay were being more subtly breached. The agent of this infiltration was, for the most, fairly nondescript in his appearance. He was wearing green hospital scrubs, which weren't too out of place since this was a hospital of a sorts. But the fact that he was wearing a face mask and a cap might have attracted someone's attention, if the orderlies hadn't been busy preventing the patients on the grounds from scurrying after the bindles of drugs strewn about. Moreover, this being a special sort of hospital, the unusual might be taken for the norm. A German psychiatrist had even encouraged patients in his care to don doctor's uniforms and assume the role of their caregivers. Inevitably, this experiment had been put to an end when a number of the patients prescribed large doses of medication for themselves.

So, advancing with a purposeful gait, his presence went unchallenged. In the room he was approaching another strange scene was being enacted. A girl in her late-teens, though dressed years younger, was playing on the floor with two figurines, a teddy bear and a robot. She grasped them tightly, "Yes roboman, those who mocked us will become our slaves and know our fury," she whispered while shaking the teddy bear vigorously.

When the door briskly opened she looked up with the eyes of a child caught doing something naughty and was about to scream at the sight of the masked figure when he spoke quickly to calm her, "Shush my daughter! I have been sent by he who has promised you an escape from this painful existence and a passage to a realm where you will be beyond all the degradation that has been heaped upon you."

"Oh, the master," she cooed softly.

"Yes the master, he has given me what you need to leave this shabby world behind."

"I am ready."

"Here it is," he took a large black pill from his pocket and she cupped her hands and stuck her tongue out as if receiving communion. She leaned back and let the pill slide down her throat. She then curled into a ball waiting for the drugs to hit her. The masked man gazed down at her at his feet as though she was a harem girl and he the sultan who could dispose of her as he wished. "It will take a while for it to kick in, probably about an hour after the limo arrives. They're supposed to take you to some kind of press conference but insist that they take you to this address instead." He then passed her a card and she took it eagerly, scrutinizing its front and back as if it might reveal some mystery regarding her fate. When nothing on either side of it seemed to give a sufficient explanation, she looked back up at the man who had given it to her.

"Don't worry, they know what to do with you."

Then, like a child basking in the appreciation of a parent, she smiled back up at the man whose identity was cloaked in a costume of healing.

FOUR

Mike reclined in the plush leather seat of the large sedan as it rolled away from the rehab center, lapsing into the detached impassive state that confrontations habitually induced in him since he'd been in combat. Suddenly, he was seized by a monstrously ill presentiment, another symptom that capriciously plagued him. The sense of impending doom was so urgent that he couldn't contain himself. "Where are we going to now?" he blurted out.

As if to reassure him, Moses let loose an insouciant burp. "Damn, that kind of action always gets the juices in my tummy flowing. We're going to my place to get rid of this piece and then back to that rehab clinic to keep an eye on that girl, she's getting out today."

"We're going to drive her somewhere?"

"No there's a limo for that, we're just going to make sure that nothing keeps the limo from taking her where she's supposed to go."

"Oh."

"What? Are you disappointed that you're not going to get to meet a star? I can get you an autographed picture of her. Oh, wait, have you ever fantasized about her?"

"About her? No way! Before she was too young and now she's a complete mess."

"Yeah, that's right, she never got you excited. That tasty piece of underage ass mewling like a kitty cat."

"No, no way."

Moses laughed, "We all have our secrets."

They soon arrived at a downtown warehouse that had been converted into dwellings. The freight elevator clanked ominously as they rode upward. Musty smells emanated from the lofts they passed. When they came to jolting halt Mike felt compelled to ask, "Do you live here?"

"Yeah, it's cheap in relation to the space and it's fortified like a bunker." He punched in a code on a keypad and slid the inner door open. "I keep a lot of things here that I don't like people getting at, like these." He walked over to a gun safe and, activating its thumbprint recognition lock, opened it to reveal an array of magnum revolvers and 9mm automatic pistols.

"Jesus," Mike intoned, "and all I got is a thirty two."

"I've got some spare cartridges here, though I'm hoping that you won't need any." He picked two boxes from a shelf. "These," he said holding up the box in his left hand, "are the blanks, and these," he continued, showing Mike the ones in his right hand, "are live rounds. I'm not going to put your print in the lock's memory just now. I've got to know you well enough." He closed the safe firmly and tugged on the handle to make sure it was secure.

"I sure wish I could have one of those automatics," Mike groaned.

"Give it some time. Meanwhile, I'm just going to add this piece," Moses pulled the P25 from his pocket, "to my masterpiece."

"Your masterpiece?"

"Yeah," Moses whipped away a tarp that covered a large object in a corner of the loft. "Ain't she something."

Mike approached the lump unsure of what he was looking at it, and as he drew near he had the feeling that something sinister emanated from it. He looked at Moses, confusion in his eyes.

"Go ahead, you can even touch it but watch out for the sharp parts."

It was not until he was close enough to touch it that Mike realized what he was looking at. What had in the distance merely seemed to be a mound of metal now revealed its component parts. It was made of thousands of pieces all welded together. Knives, guns, steel pipes and similar objects all assembled in a mass. He turned back to Moses for an explanation.

"These are all things that I accumulated in the course of my career. Actually a lot of them were simply given to me by fellow officers who heard about my project. It's all the same to me where they came from. But for some reason those that I took off a suspect on my own seem to stick out a bit, and even though this one is a piece of trash I'm going to put it right here." He tried out how the pistol fit in the chosen position and then put on a welding helmet before switching on an arc welder that was hidden behind the sculpture. After passing a hand held face shield to Mike and snapping his helmet shut, he welded the cheap weapon in place with a couple of passes.

"So what do you think?"

"They should put it in a museum."

"That'd be great but what would they call it?"

"Melting Snowman of Death."

"Melting Snowman of Death, sounds good."

"Melting Snowman of Death by the Children of an Insane Father."

"That's even better, I'll have to mark that down somewhere." Moses took a pad of paper and a pencil. "Melting Snowman of Death by the Children of an Insane Father." He then put the note book on a shelf and glanced at his watch. "We better be back at the clinic. Our client will be checking out soon."

Mike felt an unusual state of being truly present in the world overtake him on the ride back. It was as though witnessing Moses work on his sculpture had been a rite that now made him a part of the formerly unreal landscape through which he was passing. Left to wonder freely a question popped into his head. "Are we going to push our way through the crowds that will form at the gate?"

"No, officially our client doesn't want anybody 'controlling' her so we're going to keep our distance."

"So what if something bad happens?"

"Then we'll just have to try and swoop in before she gets in too much trouble."

Pulling up to the clinic they saw that forcing their way through a crowd wasn't going to be a problem. The limo had rolled through the main gates which were closed and manned by the clinic's own staff to keep the more aggressive paparazzi at bay. They continued anyway to jostle for position, trying to find a hole in the tangle of arms and legs. Moses parked the LTD and left the motor running.

Mike watched the aggressive mass of humanity squirm like some monstrous protozoa. "Glad I'm not in the middle of that."

"Well I'm sorry to tell you but we might end up in one just like it before the evening's over."

"Damn!"

"You've had crowd control problems in the field?"

"Don't ask me about it, I'm trying to forget."

"You're not going to lose it and do something crazy, are you?"

"No, no I've got it under control."

The limo backed out slowly into the street, the pack of journalists splitting in two and then surrounding it until it tore free of them and ran over several feet before rolling past Moses and Mike.

Moses turned his head keeping his eyes on it and just as it was about to be lost to his sight he pulled away from the curb and followed it downhill towards Hollywood.

Inside the limo things weren't going so well. Cheri Tarte raffled the limo's fridge looking for something. "Where the hell is the vodka? I want to make a Bloody Mary."

"Sorry," answered the driver apologetically, "we can't serve liquor to people under twenty one."

"What the fuck?" she screamed apoplectically, "do you know how big a star I am? I want some vodka for a Bloody Mary and I want it now." She spotted a liquor store. "Stop there and get me some vodka."

"I can't do that."

"Why the hell not?"

"I'm just following orders."

"That's what all fascists say."

"I'm not a fascist."

"How do I know that?"

"If I was a real fascist, I'd probably have a better job."

"Turn left at the next street."

"Left? We're supposed to turn right toward the studio for the interview."

"I don't care. You take me where I want to go or I'll jump out of this car in the middle of the road and then you'll see what sort of trouble you're in."

"But where am I supposed to stop?"

"Don't worry I'll tell you."

With a sigh of disgust the driver turned left. A few drivers honked their horns, but most, rendered diffident by the supposed status of its passenger, let the stately vehicle cut through traffic.

Moses just managed to slip by in the wake of the limo. "Damn where are they going? East Hollywood? That's even worse than West Hollywood."

Inside the limo the driver felt compelled to protest, "Where are we heading to? You're going to be late for your interview."

The pill was beginning to take effect upon Cheri Tarte, "You're not here to tell me what to do but to take me where I want to go."

The driver continued east and then turned south with Moses following. Along the way a swarm of vans belonging to different television crews gathered behind them. Moses jockeyed to keep his position. A black van with a transmitter on the roof almost cut the LTD off. "Damn, Mike keep these fuckers back."

"How should I do that?"

"Give them a harsh glare. They'll think we're with the police."

"With the police?"

"Yeah, two short haired men cruising around East Hollywood in the front seat of this mark of car? Either the police or some gay guys doing some strange type of role playing."

Mike glared with the most burning expression he could muster at the man driving the van and he backed off. "Hey, it worked."

"He obviously doesn't want to intrude upon our role playing."

Mike then turned his withering look upon Moses.

"No, I'm sorry that's one hell of a face. Scares me myself. Ha, ha, ha."

Back in the limo the drugs were beginning to take complete control of Cheri Tarte. She muttered, half to herself half to the driver, "We'll soon be there and this will all be over. All be over, all be over."

She then sprung forward out of her seat and the driver flinched as if expecting to be bitten by his crazed passenger. "Here we are, stop let me out." He braked abruptly almost causing a pile up. He let her open the door for herself and she leaped from the limo closely followed by the teeming pack of paparazzi. She ran as fast as her chubby legs could carry her toward the entrance of a tattoo and piercing parlor with the name "the Body Shop" in bright lights over a store front filled with enlarged photos of its various client's vibrantly decorated flesh.

Moses pulled over in front of the limo, "What the hell is she going to do to herself now? Some kind of damage that can't even be fixed?" He rolled forward to a side street where he parked and he and Mike got out and walked back to the shop that Cheri Tarte had entered. A grill had been pulled across its doorway, and a crowd carrying cameras and microphones pushed against it with such force that it seemed as though it might burst inward. A large man dressed all in black stood just inside the doorway trying to discourage them. "There is nothing to see right now, come back in an hour and we'll be ready for you."

Moses shoved himself through the audio-visual feeding frenzy to the grill. "You've got to let me in," he shouted to the man in black.

"Why?"

"She's my client."

"Well, she's our client now and you'll have to wait to get her back." He then stepped inside and closed the door behind the grill and pulled down a blind blocking off any view of the interior of the shop.

Fuming, Moses went back to his car. Once inside he turned to Mike. "We can't do anything while she's locked up inside that place, but we have to be ready to get her as soon as she gets out, and something tells me she isn't coming out the front."

Inside the piercing and tattoo parlor a receptionist, her skin crawling with monsters, demons, and flames led Cheri Tarte down a narrow corridor lined with more examples of the shop's work to a cramped room in the back where a man whose leather vest worn without any shirt revealed a body even more thoroughly adorned.

"Good evening, it's nice to meet you. I'm Johnny and I'm here to transform you. Everything has been made ready."

"Yeah, that's great can I have a Bloody Mary," bleated Cheri Tarte, "I'm thirsty and this asshole in the limo wouldn't give me anything to drink."

"I'm sorry but we don't have any vodka. How about some Jack Daniels?"

"Straight whiskey burns my throat."

"I think we have some cola here." He began rummaging in a small refrigerator stuck amongst the assortment of tattoo guns and surgical instruments. "Yes, here it is." He took out a bottle of Jack Daniels and a can of Coca-Cola. The receptionist held out a glass while he emptied the cola into it and then added a generous dose of whiskey.

Cheri Tarte raised the glass to her lips and downed its contents in several swallows. "So good," she sighed, "Another."

After the glass was refilled and emptied again Johnny spoke up. "We have to get down to business. The man who contacted us detailed some complex work that we have to start now." He helped her into a tattoo chair and picked up a syringe. "This will prick at first but then you won't feel a thing."

Cheri Tarte gazed dreamily up at the ceiling, "I am in your hands. Do what you must do to transform me."

FIVE

Moses left the car on a side street and came back to sit on a bench to keep the entrance of the shop under surveillance, leaving Mike in the car to call him if he saw some movement from where he was. After an hour of waiting Moses called Mike, "The feeling that she might be coming out the back door is getting stronger. Let's go look." They met behind the shop at what might have been an alley if it hadn't been blocked off by a thick wooden fence topped with razor wire. After examining it for a while he found a lock that was painted black like the rest of the fence to conceal its presence, (the alley was used by smugglers of illegal aliens to lead their charges behind the building to a basement refuge in the middle of the block). As it was a cheap lock he was able to tease it open in seconds and enter into the garbage filled passage. A bit further on they found the back door of the shop. Moses was about to knock but then seemed to decide against it.

Inside the shop Johnny had finished his work. He beamed down at the results. Cheri Tarte beckoned for a mirror to examine herself. As she admired the two large metallic horns sprouting from her forehead she smiled rapturously. "I want to show the world the new me."

Back in the alley the shouts caught the attention of Mike and Moses, "Damn I was wrong, she's coming out the front." The show was in full swing when they got there. Cheri Tarte was dancing, stripped down to a pair of bloody underpants, the horns on her head tossing wildly. She was barely visible through the grit covered windows and the grills behind them. She repeated the same set of dance moves over and over, seeming to jerk abruptly at the end of each repetition. Moses pushed his way to the front and almost instantly realized the trick that was being played upon the crowd. He forced his way back to Mike. "It's not her."

"Not her?" Mike pointed a finger at the gyrating bloody figure. "What is that?"

"It's a video loop, it must be there to keep people at the front while she....." He caught a glimpse of the speeding figure matching the one in the window but running barefoot across the filth and broken glass covered sidewalk. Mike turned his head and saw her as well. By the time they had dodged their way through the crowd she had quite a lead on them. In the distance they saw her accost a motorist filling up at a gas station. She grabbed the nozzle from his hand, and he looked on in astonishment as she doused herself with gasoline. She then staggered over to a man lighting a cigarette a few feet away and, taking the lighter from his grasp, lit herself on fire. As the fire enveloped her she ran into traffic, the video paparazzi being able to turn just in time to focus their cameras on her as she crumpled in flames.

SIX

Mike and Moses stood outside the police cordon looking at the disaster that their work had led to. Other individuals who had the luck to be less closely involved twittered and crowded in about them.

"They say it's some kind of big star."

"She burnt herself alive."

"She must of gone bat shit insane."

"Probably drugs involved."

They had been waiting amongst the gawking mass for about an hour when a fit attractive woman wearing a badge and gun on her belt approached them. "Hi, I'm Lisa Stave, LAPD homicide squad. So you are the people responsible for this mess?"

"There wasn't much we could do," Moses responded in a tone of absolution. "If a crazed individual is bent on doing themselves in, we can't do much about it."

She nodded her head in a way that said "no" even more forcibly than shaking it ever could have and then turned towards Mike, wrinkling her nose as if it were assailed by a pungent smell. "Who's this one?"

"He's someone I've taken on, a soldier, seen some combat, I think he might be useful."

"Why? Are you planning to have to fill up some more body bags?"

"Of course not, this is just some kind of freak occurrence."

"Come see the freakiness." She led them over to the body of Cheri Tarte that had been left uncovered so that the forensic team could snap photos and examine it. Her charred remains were spread out on the pitch black asphalt. "I don't know why they're always giving me the ones like this, maybe they're trying to chase me out homicide, maybe they've got a strange sense of humor or, maybe both. If it was the fourth of July she could qualify as both fireworks and a barbeque."

Moses ran his eyes over the gory sight with a look of professional detachment. "Why are you treating it as a homicide?"

"We're pretty sure that she had been given some drugs, including scopolamine. You know what that is?"

"The date rape drug?"

"That's it. We're going to interrogate the people in this tattoo and body art place and see what they have to say for themselves."

She escorted them past a team of police trying to keep the public at bay to the backroom where Johnny was being held. She flashed him a snap shot of the partially cremated remains of Cheri Tarte. "Happy with your night's work scumbag?"

"I,I,I didn't know she was going to go this far."

"Who exactly contacted you about this work?"

"Some man, I don't know his name. He sent us a check and the video loop that had been synthesized showing her dancing with the horns on her head. A video projector was sent as well. We were supposed to shine her image on the storefront shades to make people think she was still inside so she could escape out the back. I thought she was just going to cruise around the city standing up through the sunroof of her limo showing off her new look."

"She was on scopolamine, but somebody had to suggest that she kill herself."

"Right, when we had finished working on her she got a call. I didn't hear what the man on the other end said but she kept answering 'yes, yes, ok, ok.' How could I know what she was agreeing to?"

"You're going to have to give us more information than that. If we can't charge you with manslaughter, at least we can get you for criminal assault or practicing medicine without a license."

"But, but I didn't know anything about it!"

Lisa Stave turned away in disgust and led Mike and Moses back outside. A man in a blue suit with a detective's badge on his breast walked up to her and handed her a purse. She took a note from it. "Get horns in head, find gasoline, set yourself on fire, they'll be waiting for you at the filling station one block south. That's a pretty strange shopping list."

"How could they know?" Moses muttered. "How could whoever wrote this be sure that everyone would be exactly in place? The journalists out front, the man filling his car, and the other on the sidewalk lighting his cigarette."

She walked over to some patrolmen who shook their heads in bewilderment before leaning forward to consult with her in hushed tones. She then came back to Mike and Moses, "Seems the two of them took off right after she lit herself up; we're trying to track them down now."

Moses squinted his eyes as if looking at something faraway, "If they were a part of all this how could they know how to be at the right place at the right time?"

"They must have been waiting parked across the street for the moment to come. When her image appeared on the shades in the window they moved into position so she could light herself up."

"The people behind this are beginning to look like some sophisticated criminals."

"Did either of you get a good look at one of them?"

"I was too busy trying to get to Cheri Tarte to keep her from killing herself."

"Well you didn't do that too well, did you?"

"Hell, I'm not baby sitter or a nurse maid for suicidal drug addicts."

"Maybe we should go give that statement to the news, see what that does for your business."

Mike interposed himself, "I got a look at both of them. I can give you descriptions."

Lisa shot him a serious glance, "Go over to those patrolmen I was just talking to, they'll take you to the station to make a deposition."

Mike walked over and introduced himself and they put him in the car to take him to the station. Moses, who had been clever enough not to volunteer any information, got to go home to dinner and bed.

Mike looked through mug shots for several hours before being driven home. Whoever these two were, they had never been arrested before. That they were together was obvious from the fact that they took off in the same car. Though the gas stations surveillance cameras hadn't gotten a good shot of their faces, the license plates gave an address not far from the site of Cheri Tarte's death.

SEVEN

Lisa Stave decided to take Mike and Moses along with her to possibly identify the driver of the car and his accomplice. She met them at their respective abodes and drove them back towards the scene of the self-immolation and then up a hill and down the other side till they came to a street of stucco houses with stucco walls lining the front lawn of each of them. When it was freshly painted it probably had a certain charm but blackened by years of pollution it looked tawdry. They pulled to a stop in the driveway behind the car that had been used in the crime, a battered Monte Carlo that would have trouble passing its next pollution control test. Lisa led the way, going around the wall to a gate whose lock was rusted into uselessness. She gave it a push with her foot and it swung open with a creak. She mounted the red clay steps to the door and was going to knock on it when she noticed that it was unlocked.

She pushed it open slowly allowing enough light in to see two figures lying on a couch. She flicked on a light to reveal that they were both in sleeveless t-shirts with needles in their arms. They seemed too still to be alive. The table in front of them was littered with drug paraphernalia and empty heroin balloons. Lisa shook the smack heads roughly until they started to return to consciousness. They both were indignant at being so brusquely torn from the narcotic dreamland that they had been drifting through.

They didn't even seem to notice that Lisa was with the police, even after she had shown them her badge. When they were eventually roused enough from their reverie to answer questions Lisa had to keep nudging them so that they didn't drift off again.

"Are you Carlo Marcus," she prodded the one on the left. He nodded his head like a rag doll and mumbled his consent. Then she turned to the one on the right, "and who are you?"

"James" he whispered.

"James who?"

"James Marcus," he said a bit more audibly as if slowly becoming aware that the world he was leaving was not the real one but that the one he was entering was certainly it, the one with consequences and suffering, where the price was paid for the time spent in the soft, ethereal one.

"You two brothers?"

Carlo coming in his turn down off his high let out with a gasp, "Yeah, we're brothers."

"What were you doing at the gas station on Sunset Boulevard last night?"

"What anyone would do at a gas station, getting gas."

"Don't happen to remember a girl taking the nozzle out of your hand and dousing herself with gasoline?"

"What?" James said with what seemed to be a partially simulated slur.

"You know goddamn well what I'm talking about," answered detective Stave with a snarl that seemed completely genuine. "We've got it all on video tape. She got the gas from you." She pointed an accusing finger at James and then turned it on Carlo. "And she got the lighter from you." She then tossed her head at Moses and Mike, "These two saw it all."

This was followed by a hysterical deluge of mitigation, the two repeating that they hadn't known and never would have if they had.

Lisa made a placating gesture to calm the two, "Just tell me what you do know."

The two brothers looked at each other and a silent decision was made for James to be the spokesman. "He told us that it was all to be a sort of prank."

"Who told you?"

"This man, he called us up and spoke through a voice scrambler that made him sound like a machine. He spoke to me first and then to Carlo. He seemed to know everything about both of us, even that Carlo was a smoker. They told us to wait across the street and then pull into the gas station when we saw the bleeding girl coming."

Carlo decided to pipe up for himself, "He told us that it was all a publicity stunt. Nobody was supposed to get hurt."

"Yeah, but it wouldn't have mattered to a dope fiend like yourself if someone did, would it?"

"Hey no, I don't want anyone hurt. I know what pain is. That's why I have to medicate myself. I don't want to inflict suffering upon any living being. I don't even eat meat because I don't want to be responsible for animals suffering."

Lisa smiled at him wryly.

"It's the truth, look in my fridge. There's only tofu and veggie burgers and stuff like that."

"Okay, turn around, you're both under arrest, put your hands behind your head."

Having only one set of cuffs she cuffed them together, and they then fell over each other a few times before getting sat back down. James stared blankly at the torn multi-colored balloons on the table that lay there like the sad remains of a child's birthday party. "What about some medication? We're sick."

"You're sick alright," Lisa chuckled, "maybe a sympathetic prosecutor will get you into a treatment program." She turned to Mike and Moses and said dismissively, "You two can go now," and like scolded dogs they left the pathetic scene behind them.

EIGHT

For the first fifteen minutes of the drive back to Mike's apartment Moses remained silent. Mike began to feel that he somehow blamed him for the situation, not for any particular action or lack of it, but simply as a bearer of bad luck. He grew more and more uncomfortable until it was impossible to hide it, and he began fidgeting slightly with his hands and, no matter how he struggled to remain still and gaze calmly out the window, his eyes darted about. Moses decided to abridge his suffering. "That was truly a first timer for me. I mean I've had clients try to self-injure or do themselves in before but never in such a strange manner."

"Caught me by surprise as well."

"We're going to have to be on top of things from now on."

"Yeah, you're right it's just that this is new for me."

"But you must have been in all sorts of situations in Iraq and Afghanistan."

"Yeah, that sure is right. Angry crowds were the worst, but I dealt with it."

"That's good because tomorrow we've got an event that is basically a big crowd control problem."

"And you want me to be part of the security?"

"Hell, I'm going to make you assistant director of security for the event tomorrow."

"Why me?"

"I don't have anyone with any experience available, just kids. Our client slapped and spit on a police officer when she was high and now none of the off duty cops who work for me want to take the job."

"I hope she isn't going to slap and spit on me as well."

"She's doing some sort of public relations stunt to bolster her image so hopefully she'll behave better."

"Public relations?"

"I'll explain it when I pick you up tomorrow morning at nine o'clock."

They then pulled into the parking lot of the motel where Mike was temporarily staying. He left the car with a mum "See ya tomorrow" and walked up the stairs towards his room feeling ridiculed by the sheer squealing of a group aspiring actors and actresses in the pool who were playing some game with improvised rules involving a beach ball and a lot of jumping and splashing. He almost wished that he was actually aspiring to something himself and not just pretending. But then, he wondered why anyone would want to be anything at all. Maybe they were all pretending too, and doing a better job of it than him.

The following day he was awakened by Moses pounding on his flimsy door. It made the whole cheap motel room shake, and for several moments Mike thought that there was an earthquake. He didn't jump up and look frantically for shelter but simply lay there waiting to be covered with rubble. When he heard Moses' voice and realized that there was no geological event gracious enough to save him from facing another day, he rolled out of bed to greet his new employer.

"Goddamn, you're not even dressed," shouted Moses, "We got to be there in half an hour."

Mike suddenly remembered the job that was scheduled that morning. "I'll put my clothes on quick."

"Well, make it snappy."

Mike pulled on the suit and shoes that he had been wearing the day before and ran down to Moses' car. Moses looked him over perfunctorily. "Damn, why wear a suit if it's rumpled and dirty? Doesn't that defeat the purpose? Why not just dress casual?"

"I can go up and change."

"Hell no, we have to get to the site. Anyway dressing down would be better for today's assignment. It's crowd control and there might be a lot of pushing and pulling and maybe some punches thrown. People might get excited about what the crew are filming."

"Why's that? What's it about?"

"I'll bring you up to date while we're driving over there, we've got to go."

Once they were on their way Mike felt an urgent need to know what they were headed for. "So what's the subject of this shoot?"

"'Shoot?' You're going to start using industry talk now?"

"Well, what should I call it?"

"Call it what you want, it's nothing but a woman buying a hamburger."

"A woman buying a hamburger? What's so exciting about that?"

"It's that sleazy slut Madrid Ramada and she's going to be buying a Murder Burger."

"I know who Madrid Ramada is, she's the world's most famous attention whore, but what the hell is a Murder Burger?"

"It's this new burger chain that has its food named after famous killers; Bundy burger, Night Stalker shake, Son of Sandwich."

"Sounds like an insane idea."

"Yeah it is but their food is actually kind of good."

"Damn, you ate there?"

"Yeah, I had the Bundy burger. It has pieces of bacon on it shaped like a woman."

"A woman?"

"Okay, the silhouette of a woman."

"That's wild. What drove you to eat there?"

"Because I was there when the first Murder Burger became what it is. The same Murder Burger that we are going to now."

"What do you mean you were there? How did it become the very first Murder Burger franchise?"

"This was back when I was part of the force. I had taken some psychology courses at night school so sometimes they sent me out on cases where we were dealing with the mentally deranged, actually you're supposed to call them mentally disturbed but I prefer mentally deranged. A call came in that some crazy man had taken over a burger joint. It was at lunch time, so about thirty people were trapped inside with this nut case. Apparently amongst his other issues he was upset about his local fast food joint being full of foreigners."

"I got him on the phone and he started ranting about how everything was overrun by non-Americans. He was weeping when he told me about not being able to eat a meal in peace without being disturbed by people babbling on in some strange language, obviously saying bad things about him and thinking he didn't understand that he was being insulted."

"Oh, damn I heard about this case. It turned out to be a massacre."

"Yeah, and guess who got the blame."

"You?"

"That's right. I told him they would build a special burger, fries and a shake just for him, and all the foreigners would stay quiet and keep their kids from running around. I thought filling him up with this food would have an infantilizing effect upon him, and he would become passive and easy to manipulate. But I had forgotten one thing."

"What's that?"

"Those milkshakes have no milk in them."

"What does it have then?"

"I don't know, but no milk. Anyway, instead of soothing and returning him to a state like that of a baby in its mother's arms, the meal made him go berserk and gun down most of the people inside before a sniper got him with a bullet to the spine that left him paralyzed."

"Sounds pretty tragic."

"Tell me about it. He plead not guilty by reason of insanity and got out after ten years in the state hospital for the criminally insane. I almost got fired and was assigned to the ugliest jobs they had. Until my retirement I was dealing with the worst freaks and weirdos in the Hollywood community. But it wasn't such a bad thing. All that craziness got me ready to deal with the freakiness I'm dealing with now. Like this here." He nodded his head at the parking lot they were pulling into.

Wrapped up in his conversation with Moses, Mike had ceased being aware of the cityscape passing by, but when Moses brought his attention back to it he sat up in his seat as if jolted by an electric shock. They had arrived in the vast parking lot of a shopping mall and the sudden presence of so much space and light startled him. They rolled across a football field sized stretch of asphalt, approaching a large huddle of human forms struggling in the distance. As they got closer several distinct groups appeared, an angry one that pushed, agitated their arms and waved signs, a line of police holding these people back, and a third jumping joyously up and down and held in place by a smaller contingent of police.

The LTD managed to force its way through these groups to arrive at the center of their attention. Lights and cameras were being set up in a semi-circle concentrated around the side of a fast food shop painted red and black. A large sign on the roof read "Murder Burger" in dripping crimson letters. Moses parked the car and got out, followed by Mike. They stepped cautiously through the obstacle course of cables and equipment to a man who was shouting frantically at the workers setting up the material. "Damn, this should already be in place! We were supposed to be finished before the crowds arrived."

Moses approached the man but it took several long seconds before he acknowledged his presence. "Who the fuck are you?"

"Moses Murphy, Hollywood detectives."

"I'm the director. You were supposed to be here an hour ago. Now look at everything, it's all gone to shit."

"Sorry, I got held up."

"I don't know what good you'll be; the police are holding everyone back."

"Well we can look out for specific threats."

Fear filled the director's face. "What threat, did someone call or send a letter?"

"No, nothing out of the ordinary, but you can never know. It's basically something that the insurance company requests."

The director put on a disgusted expression, "Insurance companies, goddamn parasites. Just go try to make yourselves useful."

Mike and Moses turned towards the masses of humanity behind them. The protestors had pretty much been pushed back by the police, so they turned their attention to the fans who were jumping up and down like toddlers on Coca Cola.

A short obese woman with a hand drawn sign, "I heart Madrid", and a large plastic sack was particularly aggressive, jostling her blubber lined body in such a way that it seemed as though it would burst the barricade all by itself. "I want to see Madrid. I want to be near her."

Moses walked over to her, "You get too close to her and there won't be any room for anything else."

"You can't talk to me like that, overweight people got as many rights as anyone else."

The heftier individuals in the crowd pushed their way over to where she was and started shouting at Moses. He turned away so they couldn't see him laugh, and went back to where the director was welcoming the star. He was busy giving her the details of her role. "You just drive through and pick up your food."

"You know I don't usually do this."

"Well it's easy, the food will be in a sack, put the sack in the seat beside you."

"Won't it be greasy? I don't like to touch greasy things."

"It may be a little greasy but you have to act like you love the grease. When the smell of the grease hits you make like it's your favorite perfume."

"Okay, I'll try."

The director noticed Moses, "What's a matter now?"

"The fatties are getting restless."

"Oh damn, they're always a problem. They'll make so much noise we can't get decent sound. But I think I know a way to take care of them." He walked into the Murder Burger shop and several minutes later came out with some oversize paper bags.

He lugged them over to the crowd whose first rank was now flabby furies chanting, "Fat is where it's at! Fat is where it's at!" As he started tossing burgers and fries at the chubsters they shut up and began jumping after the cholesterol laden food. They were soon bouncing off of each other. The fan who had started all the trouble snagged a meal for herself from the sacks that were flying through the air and stashed it in her shopping bag. Going over to the bench of a tram stop that was not far from the fast food outlet, she gobbled down her goodies while staring up in the air at the tram's power line that past almost directly overhead.

The director came over to Mike and Moses to express his discontent, "Why do I have to take care of problems that shouldn't be mine to solve. What are you two good for?"

"Well I guess we just don't understand the masses the way you do sir."

The director held himself up contentedly, "Yes, that's why I am where I am and you are where you are."

Mike and Moses slunk back towards the crowd while behind them everything was being put into place for the first take. The sting of the director's criticism worked upon their egos as they gazed out over the exuberant masses before them. They both had the same thought in their heads, "Is this where we belong; is this what we are destined for?" If they hadn't been pondering the baseness of their role in the scheme of things, they might have noticed the source of their humiliation who was still in place at the tram stop.

Having finished her grub she was now alertly surveilling the terrain. Her pudgy hands jiggled as they urgently texted a message, "She'll be in place soon, get it ready." She then smiled mockingly at them all, the crowd, the police, the security, the film crew and the star Madrid Ramada. None of them knew what was being made ready. None of them would ever have expected it.

At the same time that the lights, reflectors and cameras were being focused upon the scene to be played, a strange contraption rolled into position on the tram's overhead line above the fat woman. It consisted of a motor, two wheels riding on the line from which it hung, a tool box size container, and a robotic grip like those used to seize hold of products on an assembly line in a high tech factory. It's metal arm unfolded as if it was reaching out for something and its fingers snapped menacingly, but nobody paid any attention to it.

Also unnoticed to all present except the lump of lard of the tram bench, an even larger mechanical arm activated on the roof of the Murder burger. In place of what would be its index finger if it had been a human hand was a metal blade gleaming sharp, ready to slice away whatever it caught hold of. It positioned itself just over the window from which Madrid was to take her deep-fried fodder.

As she reached out to take the food the grim gripper came down to trap her arm taking hold of it just below the elbow. The blade then came into play cutting her forearm off with surgical precision. She was so startled that she barely had time to scream as the steely arm extended telescopically and handed the fleshy one off to the device on the street car line.

As the two robotic hands came together a burst of smoke obscured the scene and, before it had cleared, the apparatus, holding the bloody arm, was rolling away, accelerating along the power line and dripping gore.

Though all the other onlookers were paralyzed with shock and disbelief by the bizarre and gruesome spectacle, Moses sprang into action. "We've got to get that arm. Maybe it can be reattached." A desperate glance at Mike was enough to shake him out of his state of bewilderment and they sprinted to the car, jumped into it, and took off after the amputated limb.

KILLEBRITY

This appendage was being whisked away at a significant clip. Hardly any waiting passengers remarked its passage. A steel cable that trailed down behind it to make contact with the ground was noticed by some as it whizzed along, but everyone took it for some device to test the line and no one looked up to discover its true gruesome purpose.

Moses weaved the car through an obstacle course of cars oozing along with the same sluggishness as that with which their driver's recently consumed lunches passed through their digestive tracts. None of them appreciated being roused from their torpor by Moses' honking and blinking lights. Some waved their fists and cursed the reflection of his car in their review mirrors, while others, passively resisting this assault upon their post mealtime lethargy, slowed their cars to a snail's pace.

Moses tried frantically to find a way through. The limb had already vanished in the distance and as much as Mike squinted through the smog he could catch no sight of it. "Where can they be going with it?"

"They must have some pick up point up ahead. We need to get there before they do."

"But an arm? Why an arm? What do they plan to do with it?"

"I think we've gone well past any sort of norms here. Trying to guess what is going on and why is a waste of time. We just have to get there before they do."

Eventually the majority of the automobilists turned off towards work and enough space opened up for Moses to squeeze through. Within minutes they were swerving past cars, avoiding fenders by inches. Suddenly the malefic mechanism appeared, blocked behind a tram that was traveling along the same line that it was using. Intent on following it Moses ran a red light and picked up a police cruiser that sped after him, lights blazing. Moses added up the penalties that he might incur by refusing to stop and with a "Goddamn" continued his pursuit of his client's body part.

Within a few blocks they came to an intersection where the street car turned left. To their surprise a braking mechanism inside the contraption came into play with a shower of sparks and brought it to a halt. Moses slid to a stop. He and Mike got out of the car to look up in astonishment at the strange apparatus which was still clutching the bleeding limb.

They were so dumbfounded that they paid no mind to the police cruiser that screeched to a stop behind them and took no heed of the voices shouting at them to get down on the ground, only beginning to come back to themselves after they had been thrown on the asphalt and cuffed. As the police stood them up they wondered what substance could make them stare so fixedly off into space until one of them followed that gaze and saw what the gazers saw. "What the hell? An arm?"

As he looked on, his partner went back to the car to radio in. The central informed him of the curious events that had led to this crossroads where a piece of a woman once famous for her beauty now hung like a body part of a medieval criminal who had been drawn and quartered.

Mechanically the police officer put out some calls and repeated several times the incredible facts of the situation. Eventually a vague idea of what had happened got through, and soon the intersection was buzzing with the activity of several emergency crews. They took Mike and Moses back out of the car that they had been placed in to question them about the events that had brought the arm to its place in the gizmo's grip. The pair could only shake their heads and bluntly state that they had no more insight than anyone else.

Meantime a fireman in a bucket ladder had detached the object of everyone's attention. After examining it for a moment he threw it to the ground at their feet. This action was met with howls of protest till he shouted, "It's rubber, rubber!"

And they approached only to find it was true. It was rubber, a fake. But where had the real one gone?

Back at the now almost deserted site where all the tumult had begun, the pudgy fan, who had just a short while ago clamored for some contact with Madrid Ramada, now looked down with affection at the contents of her shopping bag. "Now you are mine my beauty, now you are mine!" she repeated and anyone looking on would have taken her for another common street crazy lost in the jungle of an American city. But they couldn't see what the bag held, the severed limb of a celebrity that had been dropped down to her through the cloud of smoke that had erupted from the devilish device that had hung from the overhead line. The rubber limb which it had held concealed in its interior had popped out to call all the onlookers attention upon itself, allowing the obese devotee of a bizarre cult to hide the real one in her bag without anyone noticing. And now that she waddled away no one suspected that the bag held anything but an ordinary piece of meat, a copious cut to satisfy its bearer's ravenous appetite.

NINE

The next day the failed pair of celebrity guardians were in detective Lisa Stave's office looking sheepishly across a desk at her. She simply stared at them for several minutes trying to intimidate them into talking. Eventually she realized it was a waste of time, so she decided to speak first. "So, once again a client of yours has an extraordinary accident, any ideas as to why that might be?"

Moses raised his eyes to meet Lisa's piercing stare. "I've got a lot of clients and most of them become at some time or another the targets of deranged individuals."

"But this is different, it's some sort of strange cult-like group who for some obscure motive has decided to perpetrate these gruesome crimes. Any idea who might be behind such a group? And what motive they might have?"

"There are lots of crazies in Los Angeles and sometimes insanity is the only motive they need."

"But these crimes have been meticulously planned and could not have been the product of a severely psychotic mind."

"Well, there are some serial killers that are organized enough to plan out complicated attacks."

"Okay, but why choose celebrities as a target?"

"I don't know. Maybe they want to attract a lot of attention to themselves, and this seems like the best way to do it."

Lisa's phone rang and she picked it up. "Okay, I see, we'll take a look at it right now." She hung up the phone and turned back to Mike and Moses. "There's something on internet that I think we should watch." She turned the screen of her PC so all three of them could see it and then typed in some words. A video came up on the screen. It showed a group of hooded figures huddled around a roasted human arm.

The ghoul seated in the center of the group raised the well-cooked limb as if it were some holy artifact. With an electronically disguised voice he spoke. "Now it is time for an unholy communion. We will consume that which was worshipped by you and subsume the power that you have concentrated in her. So shall we become like stars ourselves and shine forever."

The three looked on with repulsion and stupefaction as the hooded group devoured the morsel of human flesh. Throughout the gory ritual the faces of all remained concealed and chewing sounds issued forth from the shadows that hid their identities.

Mike looked like he was on the verge of vomiting, "Who are these people? How can they do something so sick?"

Moses appeared to have lost his composure as well, "These are some seriously demented mofos."

But Lisa simply watched stoically and quipped, "If they go on like that they might just eat up all your clients, bit by bit." She then looked the two over with a solemn expression and dismissed them with a wave of her hand towards the door.

TEN

Back in Moses' loft they felt securely shut off from the world, and without a word Moses got some vodka out of the freezer. They had downed the half of it before Mike felt capable of mulling over the situation. "Do these people really believe in this whatever it is? That by killing the rich and famous and eating them they will become powerful themselves? Where will they strike next? How can we stop them?"

Moses put down his glass, "I don't know. In any organization you've sometimes got as many agendas as there are members. Especially when it's an extreme group, and if these freaks are anything it's extreme. That leads me to think that a client of ours might be the next target. She's pretty odd herself and an attack upon her might reach whatever audience this group is aiming for."

Moses walked over to his TV and turned it on. After selecting a DVD, he put it in the player. A pale elfin looking girl appeared on the screen, wearing a peculiar costume and wandering through a devastated landscape, screeching painfully to the accompaniment of discordant music.

Mike screwed up his face with discomfort, "Damn, first the cannibalism now this. What the hell is it?"

"This is Boink. Some sort of indie music star from Finland."

"What a horrible noise, how can anyone stand it?"

"Apparently a lot of people can't. It makes them go insane and kill themselves."

"Why doesn't she stop?"

Moses switched it off with the remote control, "Hell, she's making a lot of money off of it. Each time one of her crazed fans commits suicide, she goes to their funeral dressed up in some crazy costume and cries over their coffin. Makes for good publicity."

"Damn," Mike swore.

"Check out this freak," Moses enjoined while slipping another disc into the player. A morbidly obese naked man with his face and body painted in lurid colors, like that of some savage ready to go to war, stood holding a sign, "From me to you". The grotesque figure then began contorting himself as if he were dying in pain, his face grimacing like a mental patient overdosing on medication.

"I can see how she would want to be protected from that."

"She doesn't need to be anymore." Moses forwarded the video to the end where the fat freak took a revolver and, putting the barrel in his mouth, pulled the trigger. He then fell out of shot and made sickening gurgling noises.

"Okay, an example of the sort of insanity that we're going to be dealing with, is that why you are showing it to me?"

"Thing is, this nutcase offed himself here in LA. His funeral is for tomorrow. We're going to be pulling security. It's at the Forever After Funeral Home."

Mike sat around for a while trying to get drunk and talk about the situation that they had found themselves in, but no amount of alcohol or conversation could bring back the sense of reality that the last day's events had stolen from him. He tried bringing up his experiences in the military, thinking that that might draw Moses out about his life in law enforcement, but that proved pointless. It seemed as though some obscure forces much greater than themselves had put their lives on a path of chaos and destruction, and they had no choice but to wander down it to its horrible end. After an hour or so Moses gave Mike a voucher for a taxi. He rode home gazing out the window at the city, made even more hauntingly unreal by the moonlight. At his motel he laid down, planning to rest awhile before changing into his pajamas and getting under the covers, but he fell asleep without even taking off his shoes.

ELEVEN

As Mike slept, a black clothed figure with a backpack was tampering with the alarm system at the back of a single story pink stucco building whose roof swept up to a sign displaying the name of the business it housed. "Forever After Funeral Home", it shone forth in glowing neon, as if to welcome any souls that had become lost out there in the murk.

The burglar finished with the alarm and then picked the back door lock to enter the building. With a small flashlight he quickly honed in on a casket and opened it to reveal the body of the suicidal fan whose internet performance Mike and Moses had witnessed earlier that evening. He got out a scalpel and pulled up the shirt that covered the flaccid flesh to reveal the ample belly. He then cut this open and scooped out some intestines so skillfully that neither the clothes nor the inside of the coffin were stained.

Pulling a bomb from his backpack he placed it in the cavity and, after switching on a receiver on the side of it, sewed the body closed and lowered the lid of the coffin. His mission accomplished he slunk away, leaving no visible evidence of his visit.

The next morning Mike was woken by his cell phone that was ringing in his pocket where he had carelessly left it the night before. It was Moses calling. He was in his car in the motel parking lot ready to take him to the site where they were scheduled to work. Moses told him not to bother changing his clothes. "The dead don't care how we are dressed," he quipped. Mike hurried down the concrete steps to the parking lot almost stumbling a few times. He was expecting some rebuke from Moses when he opened the car door but he was met instead by the smell of coffee and donuts. Moses winked at him, "We might not be real cops but we can sure breakfast like they do."

Eating proved a good excuse not to talk and by the time they got to the funeral home the sugary treats were floating on a caffeine tide in his belly. A valet took charge of their car and they walked through the entrance that was bedecked with dyed black roses with red ribbons and shields that had writing on them in some obscure foreign language. In spite of their hue the roses gave off a sweet clingy odor. It was a bit like a passing into the afterlife of some pagan faith. The parlor where the body was displayed was surrounded by a crowd of mourners whose garishly made up faces and exotic hairdos added to the otherworldly ambience. Two men who looked like nightclub bouncers approached Mike and Moses. They were wearing black nylon bomber jackets with "Hollywood Detectives" emblazoned on the back. They introduced themselves as Fred and Rob and explained to Mike that they were there for additional crowd control. "They might go berserk and eat us," Fred joked.

Not knowing what else to do, Mike stood observing the unnatural scene. After a few minutes, a commotion started at the entrance and he went over to see what it might be. The singer Boink was coming in, accompanied by her own security crew in dark suits and sunglasses. They looked very professional and made Mike wonder what he was there for. As the crowd parted Mike could see that she was dressed in a black mini skirt, knee high black patent leather boots, and a transparent veil. As the crowd surged forward Mike tried to hold them back, but a bedraggled half mad looking woman pushed through and threw herself towards Boink shaking her fist.

"Evil bitch! You killed my son with your satanic music." The security team seized hold of her to pull her back but Boink motioned them to stop with a magisterial gesture.

"I didn't kill anyone. My music isn't evil. It's about freeing yourself, and this is the form of freedom that he chose."

"Demon!"

"I may well be a demon, but if I am one, I am a demon which won't be conjured nor controlled. I've also no need to possess anyone. I sing a music that comes to me from I don't know where. I am simply its portal to this world. If everyone was to listen to my music every day then this world would change, perhaps not for the better but it would be different. It would become the future and your son, through his extreme act, would be part of this future."

"Get out! Can't I grieve for my son without your poisonous presence?"

A thin man in a foreign cut business suit stepped forward. "I am Ms. Boink's attorney. She has every right to be here. Your son expressly mentioned in his will, sent to us shortly before his decease, that he wished for Boink to be present at the ceremony."

"But you can't throw me out either and I won't be silenced!"

Boink stared blankly at the bereaved mother, "Do as you will, scream, insult, and curse. That is how it should be."

"Satan fucker!"

Boink traipsed towards the casket.

"Hell whore!"

She bent over the body.

"Devil fornicator!"

She planted a kiss on the dead lips. Suddenly an explosion erupted from the corpse, spraying innards everywhere. The force flung Boink across the room. She hit the opposite wall and lay there barely breathing, covered in tripe.

Both Mike and Moses had been out of the path of the detonation, but they were paralyzed by the ghastly vision that it left. Pieces of the obese deceased were scattered everywhere. His blubber had liquefied and sprayed the mourners with grease and blood. Some of his intestines festooned a chandelier.

Moses shook off the shock first, "Goddamn, how the hell did this happen?" He turned towards Mike as if searching for an answer, but Mike just shook his head and looked on with his mouth hanging open. They both walked outside and stood near the entrance of the funeral parlor waiting for the arrival of teams of professionals who would come to deal with the mess. Coroners, police and a forensic team all filed past without taking any notice of them. Eventually detective Lisa Stave arrived to shake them out of their stupor.

"Yet another fiasco that you've been involved in."

Moses stuttered, "But who could have imagined that someone would do such a thing?"

"You could have done a bit more background work, examined the histories of the people that were working here. Apparently one of their employees planted the bomb. The manager is right here." She pointed to a conservatively dressed man standing at the edge of the crowd just behind the police cordon and motioned to a uniformed officer to let him pass. He stepped gingerly to them over shards of broken wood and glass, his wide opened eyes taking in the monstrosity of the scene.

"We had no way of knowing that this man was in collaboration with some terrorist group or whatever they might be. He was a licensed mortician, who had recently completed school, and came here several months ago."

"You didn't notice anything unusual about him?"

"No, he was discrete and conscientious. You know, most of us morticians are caring individuals, who would never dream of desecrating the dead in such a way. Now the employee in question seems to have disappeared. I don't know what might have motivated him to do such a thing. Oh, the scandal, I might even go out of business."

Lisa turned back to Mike and Moses. "This group is becoming more and more sinister. What can't they infiltrate?" She gave Mike an intent looking over.

Moses rose to his defense. "Hey, I'm sure that he's legit. I'm grooming him to be my personal assistant. He's back from the war trying his best to adjust to civilian life."

"Oh, why didn't he apply to be a real police officer instead of just a rent-a-cop?"

"Says he wants to make some contacts and get into show business."

She screwed up her face at Mike as if examining something distasteful, "Get into show business? Why the hell would you want to do that?"

Mike nervously searched for the words to justify himself. "I thought it might be interesting."

"Interesting? Talk to some people who work as technicians. They'll tell you it's about as exciting as watching paint dry." She paused to see what sort of effect her statement had on Mike, but he seemed at a loss for words. "I've lived in Los Angeles all my life and I never once thought about getting into show business. It attracts questionable individuals." She then turned and walked away leaving the pair to consider her parting words.

TWELVE

The next morning they met at the office to try and find a lead to the identity of the perpetrators of this heinous series of crimes. They started with an internet search. Moses entered the words, celebrity, star, hate and murder to see what came up. After clicking through several pages he found something that appeared interesting. It was a forum called "Star Bursters".

He entered a discussion page topped with a row of famous decapitated heads with their eyes gouged out. There were several hundred internauts online. "This just may be the mother lode. I'll see what the topics are." He scrolled down the page. "Here's one talking about 'Psychotropology', they're a client of ours, a mishmash of psychotherapy and religion that claims to treat people and permit them to become superior beings." The page was full of hateful threads.

"They have stopped being humans so it shouldn't be a crime to murder them."

"We should cut a few of them open to see what is going on inside and what makes them 'superior'."

"World domination is their goal, so they should be treated as any other dangerous totalitarian regime would."

Moses rubbed his forehead in consternation. "These posters are nothing but a bunch of fools. They're making themselves crazy about a group of people whose power will always be limited by their own strangeness."

Mike looked up from the page. "All the same they seem to be making quite an impact. More so than many much more reasonable groups." He reached over and clicked on a topic, "'Exterminate them all now', sounds pretty extreme." He read the opening post. "'I want to kill them all; they have destroyed my life. Their sick teachings are like a plague infecting the whole planet.' Sounds like he's not too happy with them. Look at the response, 'I am with you brother, send me a private message'."

"I'd like to see what that message says. I'm sure it's not something nice. I'm going to take you over to beef up security at the Psychotropology center."

On the drive over Moses filled Mike in on their relations with this peculiar client. "We picked up a contract with these people a couple of years ago but now I wish that we hadn't."

"Oh, why's that?"

"I don't know everything about them but they're definitely not clean."

"What do you suspect them of?"

"They use a lot of not so legit tactics to gain control of individuals and institutions: mind control, infiltration, blackmail and such like."

"So you're saying that they get their people inside of other organizations in order to take them over?"

"Yeah, they've even tried to recruit some of the employees I had working for them."

"Well don't worry they're not getting their claws into me. I've had enough indoctrination in my life, first the church when I was a kid, then the army, and after that university professors that thought the world could be changed by the writings of drug addled poets and senile philosophers."

"Damn, you have layers of resentment that are yet to be uncovered. That's one of the reasons I hired you. You seemed cynical enough not to be easily influenced by the mumbo jumbo that gets into people's heads in this town."

"Me, cynical? Hey it's all relative. Here we are going to protect one group of psychos from another. I might as well be in Iraq."

"But the thing is the psychos we're protecting here are paying us money for it."

They drove along several more blocks meditating on that statement until they came to the entrance of the Psychotropology celebrity center. Moses stopped in the driveway and nodded his head at the sign. "Most of their members are wannabe celebrities who have maybe featured in a few low budget films, TV commercials, or such like. They get them hooked when they are still small fish, and then if they ever get big they reel them in." He got out of the car and waved at a glass walled security station where a burly man in a Hollywood Detectives uniform was putting down a hamburger and standing up.

The extra-large security guard hurried over to them swallowing a morsel of food. "Mr. Moses Murphey! What a surprise. How nice of you to grace me with a visit. It gets quite boring and lonely around here."

A bit put off by the servility of his employee Moses hesitated before responding. "We've been informed of a threat to this site."

The shock registered on the man's face in such an over exaggerated manner that it recalled a child pantomiming in a class play. "A threat? From whom?"

"This whacko group that's been targeting celebrities."

"Oh yes, I've heard about the trouble. Are you saying it's all coming from the same people?"

"Apparently."

"What could be going on in their minds? I understand how people need to belong to some kind of group, but why not have it be about something like gardening or baking cakes instead of the grisly murders of celebrities?"

"I guess they're just extreme individuals and they need something extreme to get together around."

"They could be in the National Guard like me. We do a lot of heavy training preparing ourselves for combat. I never actually saw any combat though. I'm in a company set aside for domestic emergencies. I've always wanted to go to war against terror though. Maybe now I'll get to fight terrorists right here in LA."

Moses waved Mike forward. "That's why I'm bringing you my boy right here, did tours in Afghanistan and Iraq."

The weekend warrior held out his hand. "Hi, my name's Karl, proud to meet someone who's put his life on the line to fight our countries enemies."

Mike took Karl's hand. "I'm not sure you could say I did too much. Most of the time there was so much dust and smoke I couldn't see what I was shooting at. Didn't even get a confirmed kill."

"Maybe you wounded a few. Yeah, I bet there's some jihadi joker limping around right now with one of your bullets in his ass."

Mike looked at Karl's eager face with dismay and then turned to Moses. "I wanted to ask you about something."

"Fire away."

"It's about a piece of equipment in your car."

Moses looked puzzled, "In my car?"

"Yes let me show it to you."

Mike led Moses back to the LTD and they shut themselves into the already warmed interior. "I thought you didn't hire crazy people."

"He's not really crazy, just eccentric."

"Goddamn that's even worse. Most crazy people just talk to themselves. I'm going to have to spend all day listening to this guy."

"Just tell him some war stories, that will shut him up."

"But I don't want to talk about that with him. Why did you even hire him?"

"Well for one thing being a security guard isn't high on the list of people's career choices and for another I don't think that he's someone that this Psychotropology group would want to recruit. Look, just put up with him for a few days and then we'll figure something else out."

"I guess I've had to deal with worse."

"That's right, it can always be worse."

They got back out of the car and crossed the blistering hot driveway over to where Karl was standing with seemingly blissful indifference.

"Okay Mike, I'll take care of that piece of equipment and pick you up here at five thirty."

"Fine, hopefully I'll still be here."

Karl beamed radiantly. "We'll make a great team."

Mike turned away to hide his embarrassment and entered the security booth, that was thankfully air-conditioned, and sat down on a stool that seemed designed to prevent him from becoming too comfortable. Karl followed right behind, slamming the door shut to keep the cool air in. Mike feared that Karl would start right in interrogating him about his time spent overseas but thankfully he dug back into his burger and fries, leaving him several minutes of respite.

Mike then decided to speak first in order to cut off any lines of questioning that might stir up unpleasant memories. "So what's the situation?"

Karl swallowed his last bit of fast food. "Me personally I don't like to pry, so I try not to pay too much attention to what goes on here, but I believe it is definitely weird."

"Weird?"

"Yes, all kinds of weirdness. It goes on in there." He pointed across a lawn at a three story building with a gothic façade. "Take a look." He handed Mike a pair of binoculars. Mike scanned the front of the structure, the gargoyles, demons, dragons, and other creatures which adorned its surface might have looked at place on a cathedral in a European city, but here in Los Angeles seen through the prism of the heat's mirage and lit up by the southern California sun it looked like a glaring monstrosity. It seemed to be meant to warn the onlooker that some dark and loathsome practices took place within.

THIRTEEN

And at that very moment a day of what the personnel in charge called "conditioning" was being prepared. In a large white room a row of medical chairs sat facing a plexiglass booth with a complicated array of buttons and monitors. In the chairs were seated people dressed in white gowns. They all wore slightly anxious smiles on their faces. Electrodes were attached to their temples. At the control panel two men were fiddling with knobs and dials. They wore white lab coats with their titles and names on badges. That of a tall thin almost cadaverous man displayed the title of "monitor" and the name of Ralph while that of a short stooped man told that he was a "corrector" and his name was Roger.

Ralph leaned forward and, pushing a button next to a microphone, spoke into it so that his voice was conveyed to the subjects of the procedure. "You have all been prepared for this treatment that is going to help you pass on to a higher level. Positive impulses will be amplified within you while negative thoughts will be eliminated."

When Ralph switched off the microphone Roger whispered to him. "This is the first time I've helped apply this treatment. What is it supposed to do?"

"No need to whisper. They can't hear us in here. This stuff is just plain old electroshock therapy, but we bury it in some mumbo jumbo to make the suckers think that they are getting something special."

"But do we have a license to do that?"

"We've got a team of lawyers and lots of influence, so we don't have to have a license. We can do whatever we want to these chumps."

Ralph then switched the microphone back on again, "The healing will now begin." He turned a knob augmenting the voltage, and outside the people in the chairs stiffened and their smiles turned to grimaces. He then switched the microphone off, "We'll let them roast a while and go get some coffee."

Fifteen minutes later they were back in the plexiglass booth. Their electroshock patients were now trembling slightly and staring blankly in front of them. Roger looked out at them with a baffled expression on his face. "What's the purpose of this?"

"It's about breaking them down so we can then shape them into whatever we want."

"And it works?"

"Most of the time, but sometimes it drives them completely insane."

"Then what do we do?"

"Ship them off to the state hospital. We're not a charity here. If someone has no more use for us we just get rid of them."

"Sounds pretty grim."

"Well, we didn't make this world. We just try to deal with what it is. By the way did you hear about the security threat?"

"What threat?'

"It's not really clear. Anyway we have a panic room."

"A panic room?"

Ralph pointed down a white corridor towards a red door. "It's right over there. If things go bad we're supposed to run to it and lock ourselves in."

"And we'll be safe?"

"Let's hope so," Ralph the monitor whispered fearfully and looked back at the red door trying to judge how many seconds it would take him to run to it.

FOURTEEN

Meanwhile, unaware of the unethical proceedings taking place within the building they were tasked with guarding, Mike and Karl sat in the security booth and watched the traffic roll by.

Karl seemed at ease with the silence. He sat there leaning back with a look of contentment on his face surveying the passing vehicles. For several uncomfortable minutes Mike tried to ease into the same state of casual indifference as his co-worker, but he found it impossible. Recent events had combined with ugly memories to mold the world around him into something strange and frightening, where even the most innocuous object became filled with intimations of violence.

To escape this vicious ideation he was compelled to rupture the silence. But feeling the need to conceal the thoughts that were flashing through his mind as if it were a film in a projector that had been sped up almost to the point of breaking, he blurted out the opposite of what he felt, "Not much going on here is there."

Karl slowly shifted his gaze towards Mike. He seemed to know that there was something going on, but a something that was better left unacknowledged. "It's usually like that, but we have to keep an eye out all the same. Strangeness attracts strangeness."

Mike wanted to say nothing. He would have preferred keeping his distance from whatever the strangeness might be. But at the same time he felt compelled to know. What was the source of this obscure threat that seemed to hang in the air like the particles of pollution. "What kind of strangeness?"

"Do you ever ask yourself why some people are so powerful and others so helpless? Is it some kind of justice or just chance? Is it the innate qualities of the individual or the fact they belong to a particular group? Well this place here, they say they are the force that can make the helpless ones into the powerful, and so certain people are obsessed with them. Either they wish to destroy the source of what they see as unmerited privilege or wreak vengeance upon an institution that they feel unjustly excluded them."

These words comforted Mike a bit, as if no matter whatever unnatural processes were going on outside of the security booth, he was in some way insulated from them. This led to a feeling which had grown foreign to him. He wanted to get to know Karl. It wasn't exactly friendship he was looking for, friendship was a feeling that had become impossible for him some time ago. He simply wanted for a short while to see the world as others saw it and escape from the hideous cage of ugly thoughts that he felt trapped in. He decided to use flattery to solicit Karl and reveal whatever thoughts might be behind his rather plain looking face. "I see. Say you seem like an intelligent guy, how did you end up working in security?"

"Chose the wrong major in college."

"Yeah, I guess I did as well. What major did you choose?"

"Philosophy, asking questions about why we exist, it's good for nothing but making you sick in the head."

"You don't think it might prove useful?"

"No, not all ideas are useful to all people. You have to have a way of understanding things that matches the way you're going to live your life. If you are going to live a dull and servile life you have to somehow learn to feel as though it has a sense. That there is something out there, a political party, a pop music group, a sports team etc. that makes it all seem as though it's worth it. To know that all these things are nothing, and you are living your life like a morsel of food being slowly digested will make it all unbearable."

"Wow."

"Anyway," he patted the nine millimeter in the holster on his belt. "I've always got the solution right here."

Mike began to feel that maybe he had made a mistake. Maybe he didn't want to know what was hidden in all the nooks and crannies of the brain of the man seated next to him. "Sounds extreme," he muttered timorously. He made a clumsy attempt at levity, "At least you've got what it takes to do the job."

Karl pulled the automatic pistol slowly out of its holster and studied it. "Yeah, this is sure to do the job." He then put it carefully back. "What kind of piece did Moses give you?" Mike passed him the thirty two caliber revolver he'd been provided with. Karl gripped its handle and sighted down its barrel before handing it back. "He gives this piece to all the new guys just to put them in their place. But I'm a senior employee so I equip myself."

"Oh."

Karl pulled a duffel bag out from under the desk and took out a Chi-com AK47 with a thirty round clip to show Mike.

"Aren't those illegal?"

"I got it before the ban, and besides I'm in the National Guard."

"I didn't much like the army myself, the training, the discipline."

"Oh? Do you do the manual of arms in the same way as we do?"

"Yeah, I think so."

"Well let me show you." Karl stood up. "Left shoulder arms," he shouted out and brought the assault rifle to his left shoulder. "Right shoulder arms," and he brought it to his right shoulder. "Present arms," he thrust the AK 47 out in front of him and lunged forward slamming the stock into Mike's chin knocking him out. He then administered several gratuitous blows to Mike's head. After nudging Mike with his foot to make sure he was completely unconscious, Karl detached the thirty round clip and, picking up a seventy five round drum magazine, snapped it into the receiver.

Meanwhile inside the Psychotropology center Roger and Ralph were watching their clients get their brains fried. They barely paid any attention to Karl when he came in as he had his AK 47 with its drum magazine concealed inside his sports bag and wore such an idiotic grin on his face.

But his words and the teasing tone they were pronounced in did not reassure them. "Nice day for a barbecue." Ralph instantly thought that Karl was trying to get close to the processes that were underway in order to interfere with them or gather evidence that might be released to the public to discredit them. The employees of the center were frequently warned about the danger of intruders and the necessity of keeping the center's activities secret from them.

He became instantly aggressive, "You're not supposed to be here! We're conducting a very sensitive operation!"

A sneer on his face, Karl took in the chamber that he had never before entered. It matched fairly closely the image he had formulated of it, a layperson's idea of a laboratory where important research might be carried out, but to Karl's informed eyes it looked as phony as a low budget movie set. Machines that were connected to nothing made strange noises and shone with a mysterious light. The patients or subjects or whatever they might be called were maintained in a state of artificial unconsciousness without any of the apparatus necessary to insure they didn't slip into a coma. A white canopy hung over the entire space which, while providing a certain new age ambiance, also presented a serious fire hazard.

Karl took it all in and, though the goofy grin remained, his eyes filled with rage. "Bullshit, what the fuck are you really doing to these people?"

"We are modifying their brain waves."

Karl sneered, "I've got an easier way to do that." He pulled the AK 47 out of its bag and sprayed bullets at the limp human forms in a neat head level line. Their brains splattered the wall behind them. Roger and Ralph had jumped back in fright upon sight of the weapon and then remained frozen like baby bunnies lost in the woods while Karl casually executed their former charges. As Karl slowly turned towards them they snapped out of their state of shock and fled towards the panic room. Karl followed their flight through the sights of his gun anticipating cutting them both in two but as he pulled the trigger nothing happened. He cursed himself. He had wanted this day to be special and so he had hand loaded all of the rounds. Bad time to find out he wasn't as skilled at loading as he had imagined. He'd fired thousands of rounds through this very weapon without any problems, so it had to be the ammo. He racked another cartridge into the chamber and rushed towards the door that his quarry had disappeared through.

He tried shooting through the door but the bullets ricocheted back at him. One even nicked his shoulder and gave him a flesh wound. He cursed at the blood that streamed out, "Mother fuck!"

Inside the two pseudo medical technicians cowered in fear. "He's going to kill us," Ralph blurted out.

"Stay still and be quiet," exhorted Roger. "I'm calling the police right now."

With a trembling hand he managed to fish his mobile phone out of his pocket and after desperately stabbing his finger at the keyboard for several long seconds he succeeded in entering the number 911. "Hello, I'm at the Hollywood Psychotropology center and we've got a serious problem." He listened to their response his lips quivering so energetically that he seemed to be intoning a silent prayer in some high speed language. After hearing what they had to say his pale faced terror began to take on a rosier tone, but he felt obliged to repeat what he had been told to reassure himself. "Someone already called you! Help is on the way!" He hung up and turned to Ralph. "We are saved, thank Cthulhu, we are saved!" He then turned towards the door his ears rising and twitching like a small forest creature listening for a fox. "He's stopped shooting; he must not have any more bullets."

Unbeknownst to the trio behind the door, Karl had several full clips left and had stopped firing simply because he had noticed it wasn't producing significant results. But, like the good boy scout he had once been, he was always prepared. Not only did he have plenty of ammo in his bag he also had some explosives that he'd bribed a fellow guard member in a demolition brigade into giving him. He smiled wickedly as he fixed the door to implode.

Ralph and Roger had just sat down on a sofa to await the arrival of the police when the blast threw them to the ground. They lay semi-conscious on floor, their limbs akimbo like corpses on a battlefield.

Karl strode threw the ruined smoking entryway like a conqueror and surveyed the scene at his feet with disdain. "So I see you creeps thought you could hide from me?" He studied them closely, the barrel of his AK 47 following the movement of his eyes like they were both part of the same precision machine.

With a supplicating look Roger raised his eyes to meet Karl's malevolent glare. "I know that what we are doing must seem unusual but it is meant to help people."

"Help people? This stuff is nothing but a sick joke."

"But you have to understand, our patients have troubles that are buried deep inside them. We must use extreme measures in order to root the sickness out."

"Extreme measures?"

"Yes and we can help you as well. Not meaning to give any offense, but you obviously have much anger lodged somewhere in you, and with our techniques we could remove it like a surgeon operating on a tumor. Then you would be freed from this negative emotion, free to live a happier life."

Karl rolled his eyes up towards the ceiling like a martyr recipient of a heavenly vision, "Free from all the hate and ugliness."

"Yes! Yes! Free! We shall cure you!"

Karl chuckled and the leered evilly at his would be savior, "I think I know a better, simpler way to get all the badness out of this head." With a short burst he tore the bodies of Roger and Ralph apart as if he was working on them with a chainsaw, then, putting the barrel in his mouth and not even wincing as his lips touched the hot metal, he blew apart the troubled tissue of his tormented mind.

FIFTEEN

By the time the twisted scene inside the clinic had reached its bloody denouement the synapses in Mike's bruised and swollen brain were reconnecting well enough to bring him around to a fuzzy state of semi-consciousness. The force of the blow had erased the memory of the events leading up to the knockout. He lay there on the floor not knowing what had happened, but his imagination filled those missing minutes with all sorts of possible terrors. As unsure as he was of what had happened, he was certain that it was something bad.

As he managed to roll to his knees the approaching sirens confirmed his fears. The sound of them going in and out of sync as if they were on discs spun by some ketamine crazed DJ invoked the image of a horde of emergency vehicles converging. He wanted to get up to be prepared for their arrival, but his head swam when he tried to get any higher than his knees.

He was afraid that he'd be taken for some culprit who was lying concealed in the booth in order to ambush the teams of emergency responders. His fears were confirmed when a fist banged aggressively on the side of the transparent structure and a voice shouted, "Come out with your hands in the air."

Straining his voice to the maximum he managed to croak, "I've been injured. I can't get up!" There was a loud bang as the lock was blasted away and the small space filled with smoke. He passed out again to wake up face down on the pavement near the entrance. A man in a SWAT uniform was bending over him.

"How many shooters are there?"

"Shooters?"

"Yes inside! Someone opened fire and blew some things up, a terrorist attack." The well-armed and armored man rolled him over so he could yell straight into his face through a plexiglass mask.

The aggressive tone of the officer compounded Mike's confusion. Had he blacked out? Done something bad? What the hell had happened? "I don't know," he stammered. "I just woke up here." With a hostile look the officer rolled him over so roughly that he banged his head and passed out again.

He woke up on a stretcher with an emergency blanket wrapped around his shoulders. His hands were free but still bore the marks of having been tightly cuffed. He rubbed his wrists and peered upward to see Lisa Stave looking him over.

"Do you know what happened?"

"No, no, I just remember coming here then it's all a blank." He felt the back of his head. Most of it was covered by a bandage and where it wasn't his hair was sticky with blood. He held the red stained fingers in front of his face seeming to wonder how they'd gotten that way.

"You were supposed to be working here today, yourself and another security guard named Karl."

Mike squinted his eyes as if trying to bring the blurred past into focus. "Yes, I think I remember Karl. He was some kind of philosopher or something."

"A philosopher? Did his philosophy include going berserk and killing a lot of people?"

"Killing people? I remember a gun, an AK 47, I wondered why he had brought it here."

"Did you know Karl?"

"Know Karl? I don't think I understood him."

Lisa stared intently at Mike trying to figure out if it was just an act. His eyes didn't meet hers but instead roamed randomly about, like those of a newborn child for whom seeing is still a task it's learning to master. She decided a medical opinion was needed and went to get a paramedic. A short examination confirmed that Mike had been hit extremely hard several times and suffered from a severe concussion and multiple cranial fractures. Mike was barely aware of being trundled away on a gurney and loaded into an ambulance. The last thing he remembered was a bright light shining painfully into his eyes so hard that the heavy darkness that followed was a blessed relief.

When he started to come out of it he could feel that he was being observed by a group of people. He didn't want to face them and he thought about feigning sleep to avoid whatever sort of unpleasantness was awaiting him in the world of the conscious, but he knew that they weren't going to go away. A voice with a technical tone affirmed his fears, "He should be coming around now." And feeling that he had no choice, Mike slowly opened his eyes.

The first person he saw was Moses, who looked concerned. Concerned about what Mike wondered. That a recently hired employee had gotten his head bashed? He didn't seem like the sort of person to let something so trivial unnerve him. Then he heard detective Stave's voice calling out to the left of him. "Mr. Johnson, are you awake? I'd like you to answer some questions."

He had to painfully turn his head to look at her. She was seated to his extreme left. She could have easily slid closer to him but held herself poised at the edge of his sight. He wondered if she had purposefully stationed herself there as some sort of interrogation strategy. "Yes, I think so. I feel a bit strange. Something happened, I don't know what, but I think it was something terrible."

"Yes it was something terrible and we'd like to know how you were involved."

"Involved? How? The last thing I remember is Karl showing me his gun, an AK 47, and then I think he hit me in the head. I woke up on the floor of the security booth."

"So what do you know about Karl?"

"Not much, I don't know why he knocked me out."

"You never met him before?"

"No."

"We found this card in your wallet." She held up the Hollywood Detectives card that had mysteriously gotten into his pocket. "Might you be able to tell us how you got this card?"

A burning uneasiness began to overwhelm Mike, as if he were suddenly standing judgement for all the errors of his life. "I, I, don't remember. It was just after I'd gotten back to the States, I'd been drinking heavily and I woke up one morning with that card in my pocket."

"That doesn't sound very plausible."

"What difference does it make? It's just a card."

"Just a card?" She turned the card over and read the writing on the back of it. She recited it slowly and distinctly as if presenting evidence in court. " 'I think this would be the right place for you at least until you get back on your feet'. Do you remember who gave this to you?"

"No I haven't the slightest recollection. I must have been so drunk that I blacked it all out."

"A blackout? Do you often have blackouts?"

It was as though he was being accused of thousands of horrible acts, none of which he had any memory, all of them committed while he was drunk. "When I came back I went on a binge."

"Do you remember what you did during this binge? Who you might have met?"

"No, not at all it's all a gaping black hole."

"But you must have met at least one person, a person who gave you this card."

A queasiness began rising in Mike, as if the dose of the liquor he had imbibed during that lost week had lain fermenting in his stomach and now was churning inside him. "I must have."

Waving Moses out of the way as if he were a cloud of smoke she rolled the chair over to the bed with a thrust of her legs. She took a log book out of an evidence bag and then slid to a position where she was hovering right over his mouth like a dentist. "This is the log for the Psychotropology site." She opened the log and held it up to his eyes. "See the entry?"

"Yes."

"Now look at the signature."

He scanned through the page full of precisely written little letters denoting the routine passage of various personnel and delivery men till he came to the end where the writer had left his mark, the same extravagant "K" that was written on the back of the cryptic card that had led him to where he now found himself. "Oh, no, it can't be, it's all some kind of trick."

"A trick? Yes, but played by who?"

"I don't know. Who'd do something like that?"

Detective Stave swiveled in her chair to glare at Moses. "Do you encourage your employees to recruit drunks in dive bars to work for you?"

"Actually, I try to avoid hiring people based on acquaintanceship."

"Did you know that Karl had met Mike?"

Moses shook his head vehemently, "Nope I had no idea whatsoever. I thought Mike had heard about us by some other means."

She turned accusing eyes towards Mike, "We've no one to explain this but you, and you say that you blacked everything out. I don't know if and how you were involved but I'll find out."

Tom stuttered in protest, "I, um, well."

He was interrupted by a policeman in uniform who suddenly appeared breathlessly at the entrance. "They're all dead, a dozen of them," he blurted out.

Detective Lisa Stave nodded gravely. "The perpetrator was out to kill everybody. For some reason he let this one live. We'll find out why later." On that menacing note she stalked out of the room and a nurse came in to treat the confused and injured man. As his wounds were inspected Mike wished the damage had been worse, that he had been so badly beaten that no one could accuse him of any complicity in Karl's rampage.

Then, either as a delayed reaction to the blow, or because of something he was injected with, or perhaps a combination of the two, he slipped into a deep state of unconsciousness. He sunk into a dark and threatening place where he relived the ugliest parts of his past. His father, his eyes blazing with anger, beating him savagely. His mother in the mental institution zoned out on anti-psychotic medication. Tracer bullets searching him out as he hugged the sand. Finally he found himself in some bar with Karl sitting next to him. The recently deceased bought him a drink and passed him a business card before vanishing.

Mike woke up on the hospital bed wondering how he had gotten there. The nightmare had been so vivid that it blanked out the recent horrifying events. He sat up and noticed he was handcuffed to the bed. He rattled the bed frame by pulling futilely on the cuffs. As if summoned by a bell Moses stepped into the room. He squinted hard at Mike, "We have to have a serious discussion about a number of things." Moses breathed in, filling his lungs with enough air to supply the lengthy diatribe he was planning to launch, when he was suddenly interrupted by the entrance of a tall pale man in a dark suit with a dour expression on his face. Moses stepped back into the corner with resignation and the man placed himself at the foot of Mike's bed.

"I'm detective Mark Ruh."

"Oh, I'm under arrest?"

"For the time being."

"For what?"

"Complicity to commit murder."

"Murder? But I didn't help kill anyone."

"You knew Karl."

"Not really, I had met him."

"So now you admit meeting him."

"Yes, I remembered just now when I was out. It was a chance encounter."

"Now you remember. A chance encounter. That's convenient."

"The memory of what had happened was lost in some part of my brain. The blow to my head must have shook it out."

"If you're planning to plead insanity then maybe we should call the doctor in."

The detective left in search of a medical opinion and Moses and Mike were alone again. Moses didn't say anything to Mike, simply giving him a long hard look that made him more uncomfortable than any words might. Thankfully, detective Ruh soon returned with an astute looking man, hunched over with age and grasping several folders to his chest. With a deftness that belied his elderly appearance, he pulled out a sheaf of x-rays and stuck them up in a viewer that was besides Mike's bed. He then spread a bunch of photos out on the nightstand and reached over to Mike to smile broadly and shake his hand vigorously as if he was the winner of a prize. "Good to see you're recovering, I'm Doctor Friedhof," he said in a voice without any accent but too clipped and precise for an American.

Moses and the detective had apparently been introduced to him already. He pointed towards one of the x-rays and waved the two over to where they could see. "You see this?" They both squinted at the place in the image but didn't seem able to make anything out. "This small line here is a hairline fracture of the skull."

"Yes, okay I see," the detective admitted. "So what does that mean?"

"Right here is the one of the hardest places of the skull. And right here and here," he exclaimed while jabbing his finger at two points beside the fracture, "are the weakest."

"Right, I've studied anatomy a bit. What are you trying to say?"

"That madman who killed so many people could not be in cahoots with our friend," he waved his hand at Mike, "lying here." He picked up the photos from the nightstand. "When you see these," he spread them out like a losing hand of cards and they winced a bit at the sight of Mike's torn and bloody scalp. "You can see that this murderer beat my patient while in a frenzied state. It's only by pure chance he wasn't killed."

Detective Ruh stepped over to the window facing out into the hospital corridor and looked out at the people hustling by. He stood there, back to the room, thinking for several minutes before facing the others again. "So if he wasn't part of the massacre then what was his connection with this Karl maniac?" Everyone was obviously as puzzled as he was. He stood there at a loss as to what to do. As if in response to their disarray, his phone rang out.

He pulled it out of his pocket and answered without even glancing at the incoming number, "Detective Ruh here what can I do for you? Oh, I see you've turned the whole place over. What did you find? I see, he left some surprises for you. Was it dangerous? No one got hurt? So it can't be him. I see." With a mirthful little snort he put his cellphone away. "That was Lisa Stave. Apparently Mike here was somehow a target of Karl as well. He picked him out and set him up, approaching him when he was too drunk to remember it and passing him the card for your 'security agency'." The detective threw Moses a derisive smirk then went to the bed to recover the handcuffs attaching Mike to it. "Why he wanted him to work for you is still a mystery. We'll have to figure this out later." Sauntering nonchalantly out of the room he gave them a backwards wave of goodbye.

SIXTEEN

Moses began pacing back and forth in the little space available in Mike's hospital room. Mike wanted him to just say he was fired and get it over with. When he thought about it he came to the conclusion that he didn't really belong in the workforce or anywhere in society. The papers he had signed made him ineligible for a military pension, but he might qualify for social security disability. Then he could get a room in an old hotel in downtown Los Angeles and just drop out of the whole circus. The idea of reclining in a bed in some dump full of derelicts and doing nothing all day but drinking cheap booze began to seem kind of attractive to him.

His reverie was interrupted by the cacophony of Moses clearing his throat. It went on for some time and began to sound as if something was lodged in his trachea choking him. Then the raucous noise suddenly stopped. Perhaps it had all been for dramatic effect, like the discordant horns that introduced a speech by a pagan king in a sword and sandals movie. "I should fire you."

"Yes, I understand."

"No, you don't. I said should."

"But what, you aren't going to?"

"No, these people or this person or whatever it is that is doing all this sent you to me. I want to know why. Keeping you around seems like the best way to do that. First I need to know why you came to me."

"I needed a job that's all."

"Why this story about wanting to meet the right people become an actor and all of that?"

"I felt I needed a reason."

"A reason? A reason for what?"

"A reason for being, for being how I am."

"Being? Being how you are? How are you?"

"I don't know. Most of the time I feel like I don't even exist. Except...."

"Except when?"

"Except when I'm drunk. In a crowded bar. Then I feel just like any other person, but they stay away from me like they know I'm not like them."

"What did the military doctors say?"

So there it was, Moses had cut through it all right to the disturbing truth. Mike had no choice but to come clean. "One said that I had posttraumatic stress disorder. Another said that I had a preexisting psychotic disorder that had been triggered by the stress of combat."

"How did they resolve that?"

"They had me sign a paper saying that I wouldn't seek any kind of financial remuneration, and in return they promised me a normal honorable discharge instead of a medical one."

"You didn't want a medical discharge?"

"No, the idea that that would follow me around for the rest of my life was too much."

"So instead you end up working for me? Great!"

"It wasn't something I planned."

"No, you're not in a state to plan something like that. But you made a useful patsy and made me look like a fool."

"I'm sorry. I wish I could make it up to you."

"You can. Of all the people that have been made use of by this ugly organization you're the only honest one left alive. That can be of help."

"How?"

"I don't know but I'll find a way."

They both quietly wondered what that way might be for several minutes until Detective Stave brusquely swung the door open letting the hubbub of the busy hospital corridor in to break the silence. "I've found out a lot of things in a short period of time, all of them very peculiar." She held up a folder and looked through it with eyes full of incrimination. "This is about the most twisted series of crimes I've come across and both of you seem to be caught up in it somehow."

Moses raised his hands as if surrendering, "We didn't know anything. We still don't."

"You better get to work finding something out. We can't let you stay in business if this deadly cult or gang or whatever is using you to help target its victims. Goddamn, you're supposed to be protecting these people but instead you're getting them killed."

Moses looked down, scanning the floor for several long seconds as if some answer to his predicament might be found there in the pattern of the linoleum. He then nodded his head as if some sort of understanding had come to him and looked up towards detective Stave with cold resolve. "This organization, whatever it is, has to have started somewhere. Seeing that they seem to have an obsession with my clients leads me to wonder if the instigator might not be someone who I had some contact with in the past. Someone who's still harboring resentment towards me. I'm going to look up some old cases and see what that leads to."

"Well you do that. But you better keep me up to date. I'm going to be following the activities of both of you." She surveyed Moses and then Mike and then Moses once again all the while pursing her lips with what appeared to be scorn. "Happy hunting 'gentlemen'," she chortled with a mocking smile and sashayed out of the room leaving both of them lost and puzzled.

Before Moses could compose a speech to advise Mike as to what the future of his employment might be, a nurse came in and shooed him out. In parting he declared, "In four days, when you get out, we'll go after some answers." Mike's reply was nothing but a weak nod of his head, but even this slight movement did something to his damaged cortex that caused him to drift off.

The rest of Mike's stay was thankfully free of any visits besides the doctor and a few nurses. He appreciated the calm and found himself almost looking forward to his dying days which would hopefully be passed as tranquilly. He awoke on the fourth morning of his stay to find the doctor peering at him. "So everything better? I think we can let you go."

Mike was seized by a sudden fear of the outside world. He stammered, "Are you sure I might not need a few more days here?"

"No, no, sorry we need the bed for those much more unwell than you." He then popped out of the room and Mike lay waiting until a nurse came in. She gave Mike back the clothes he had come in with, the still bloodstained uniform, and waited on the other side of a screen while he got dressed. She then placed him in a wheelchair and after wheeling it through a maze of corridors rolled him out of the entrance to where Moses was waiting for him at the wheel of his LTD, the motor running. A muscular security guard with a heavily Slavic accent was berating him for parking in a pick-up zone. "This is pick zone, you no park here."

In a hurry to get in the car and avoid a scene Mike stood up too quick and almost fell down when his head started turning. Luckily the nurse steadied him and got him buckled into the front passenger seat. Moses bawled at the man, "See what you did? He could have gotten hurt because of you!" Putting the large car in gear he swung aggressively away from the curb almost running the man over.

In the rear view mirror Moses watched him shake his fist into the trail of car exhaust and then chuckled. "Mofo doesn't even remember me. He applied for a job with us a few months ago but he was too literal minded, the type who fantasizes about being a cop but doesn't got what it takes. You see we don't hire just anyone."

Moses' last statement hung uncomfortably in the Freon treated air. Mike shuddered but he put it down to the chill. "You do like to turn up the air-conditioning," he murmured wrapping his arms around himself.

"I like it cool. Spent a lot of time on surveillance with the motor off. Feels like my body is still sweating. You'll get used to it. We've got a long drive to make. Take a beer from the cooler in the back."

Mike reached around and pulled out a bottle, "Rolling Rock, my favorite."

"You see, how did I know that?"

Mike squirmed a bit in his seat and looked around for a bottle opener. "I don't know. How?"

"Said on your resume that you lived back east for a while, spent some time in Pennsylvania. Everybody who's lived there knows Rolling Rock's the best."

"Yeah, that's right."

"So why did you move around so much?"

"I don't know. Sort of felt that somewhere else might be better."

"But it never was, was it?"

"No."

"I've met all kinds of vagabonds. Like the man we're going to see. But he isn't moving around much anymore. They've got him in Barkersville prison now and I helped put him there."

"Barkersville? That's in the central valley."

"That's why the cooler with beer and some sandwiches. Got a thermos full of coffee for myself."

"But my clothes. I've got this bloodstained uniform on."

"So much the better, looks like you just got back from the front."

"What front?"

"The front of whatever war we're fighting." Moses gazed grimly out at the mass of traffic oozing along. "Goddamn DMV gives out licenses too easily, most of these idiots don't even know how to drive. In a lot of countries they couldn't even pass the test."

"Well, it's LA, they're not going to accept taking mass transit. Mass transit is for losers here. If you tell someone you don't have a car it's like saying you're no longer human."

"Christ, I'm going to end up taking mass transit myself when these whack jobs destroy my business. I had a feeling that bad things were going to start happening, that's the reason I hired you. You've been to college and in Iraq. I thought you'd have some solutions when the shit came down."

"One thing I learned in Iraq is that there are no solutions. The problem is something inside of people, and unless you want to exterminate the human race then the problem isn't going away."

"Damn, you're a cynical fucker."

"Maybe it hasn't made me popular but it's kept me alive."

Mike took a swig of beer and settled back in the plush leather seat. He finished his beer and then drank a few more. The traffic dissipated and soon they were cruising along through bland beige hills. The monotony of the landscape lulled him into a drowsy state where time passed fleetingly. Before he noticed the hills had given way to a vast flatland with oil pumps pecking at its scraggy surface like relentless parasites.

SEVENTEEN

A few beers later they turned off the state highway onto a county route, and a festively colored sign arcing over the asphalt appeared, marking the frontier of their destination. "Welcome to Barkersville" it proclaimed joyously while in every direction there was nothing to be seen but more wasteland. As they continued, a complex of gray, concrete bunker like buildings appeared in the distance. Soon guard towers and fences became visible through the mirage rising from the baked earth.

They continued past the well-fortified prison entrance and entered the town of Barkersville itself. Following a potholed street lined with trailer parks full of weeds and the rusting hulks of recreational vehicles they came to what was left of the desolate hamlet's center, shop fronts that were mostly boarded up except for a few that looked like they specialized in selling alcohol and junk food. As they stopped at what was probably the town's only traffic signal the first sign of habitation manifested itself.

A worn out mid-seventies dodge sedan eased stealthily up behind them. On its roof were a siren and red and blue emergency beacons that looked years out of date, and it sported a cheaply applied matte gray paint job. When the light turned green and they rolled on the signals on the odd vehicle lit up and began gyrating and wailing. Moses pulled over to the cracked, trash strewn sidewalk and rolled his window down, allowing foul torrid air to gush into the car. He gripped the wheel to keep from flinching and tried to catch a glimpse of what was going on behind him in the rear view mirror. The occupants who emerged from the junky police car were even rougher looking than it was.

Wearing dark tattered clothes that might once have been a janitor's uniforms, they crept towards the car their faces hidden in the shadow of their wide brimmed hats and their hands on the butts of their revolvers. They spread apart, each of them approaching one side of the car. The one on the driver's side leaned toward the window. A fetid smell of stale sweat emanated from the squalid law officer. "Where you boys going?" he drawled with breath even worse than his body odor.

"To a motel."

"What motel? Are you two tourists?" He stood up to address his partner, and the movement liberated an even stronger stench of filthy clothes and unwashed flesh. "Maybe we got some love birds on their honeymoon?" He chuckled displaying badly decayed teeth. Still smiling he bent back down towards Moses. "Is that it? You two looking to pass a romantic interlude in our beautiful burg?"

As stoically as possible Moses answered, "We're meeting someone."

"Oh, what? For some kind of business? A criminal enterprise maybe? Drugs? Whores? We find that stuff real fascinating."

"No, we're visiting someone in the penitentiary."

"Don't say." He stepped back to survey the car then stuck his face back in the window. "So you LAPD? Up here to talk with an informant?"

"Ex-LAPD, I own a security service now."

"So, like chief of the rent-a-cops? That don't carry much weight around here."

"I've come to talk to Thomas Barker."

At the mention of the name the two of them sprang back and pulled their guns shouting in unison, "Out of the car hands on your head." They then opened the car's doors with one hand while aiming their weapons at Moses and Mike with the other. After guiding the pair to the pavement and cuffing their hands behind their backs, they proceeded to pat them down. The one searching Moses plucked his wallet out of his pocket and finding a business card read it out loud. "Moses Murphy CEO Hollywood detectives, that's you?"

Moses raised his head from the sweltering pavement, "Yeah, yeah that's me."

Before the cop standing over Moses could interrogate him further the other one suddenly stood up and shouted out, "This one has dried blood on him."

He then trained his gun on Mike with both hands. "Where did that blood come from?"

"I was victim of a crime."

"A crime, what crime?"

"A massacre."

The cop covering Mike took his left hand off the butt of his gun to stroke his scraggly goatee, "A massacre? Where? In LA?"

"Yes, at the Psychotropology center."

The unkempt cops looked at each other with child-like surprise on their dirty faces. For several long seconds they seemed at a loss for words. Both Mike and Moses lay where they were fearing the response that this revelation might bring. What sort of justice could they expect from this motley pair?

Putting his gun away the goateed one rendered a verdict. "We saw it on the news. You're a hero!" He helped Mike up and took his cuffs off while the other did the same to Moses. "You're lucky to have survived. Already back on the job are you?"

"We're trying to figure out what happened."

"But why here? Why Barkersville?"

"We wanted to talk with Thomas Barker."

The dingy duo exchanged startled looks and the rotten toothed one spurted out, "Tommy, they want to talk to Tommy." Their faces grew blank and pale and Moses was starting to worry that he might have said the wrong thing when the goateed one spoke to them with a starry eyed look and an adolescent voice, "Go to see Tommy, he has all the answers."

"Yes, Tommy. The truth." intoned his partner reverently. Then, in a more earthly manner, he stated, "You two will need a motel to stay in, got reservations?"

"No," Moses answered shaking his head, "we left in a rush."

"Well, let us show you the way to the friendliest place in town."

Not wanting to question their recent detainers' judgment, Mike and Moses got back in the LTD and followed the beat up police cruiser. They rolled past rundown cheaply built houses on streets empty except for the occasional homeless looking person shuffling along.

Mike felt obliged to ask, "What the hell is this place?"

"Just wait until we're in the motel, then I'll explain," Moses replied.

After a short drive they arrived at their accommodations, whose name, "Majestic Motel", was displayed on a neon sign flickering futilely in the blazing sun. It didn't look like a place for welcoming royalty, but, with its cinder block walls brightly painted pink and its recently refurbished asphalt roof, it looked much more habitable than any other structure they had passed.

The driver of the cop car waved his arm towards it then drove on. Moses parked the car and the two of them went to the reception. A window slid open and a cheerful teenage girl with a shaved head and a ragged shirt greeted them. "Hi, welcome to Barkersville, the town of tomorrow."

The two of them stood there grimly reflecting on the fact that maybe the future would look like the desolation they had just passed through. But cheerily the receptionist broke their chains of thought before they became too dark. "You two gonna stay with us? I'll find the right room for you."

"The right room?" Moses queried.

"Yes, numbers are important. Wouldn't want to give you the wrong room number. That could be a catastrophe."

"We've had more than our share lately. What do we do to get the right number?"

"Give me your ID." They handed over their driver's licenses and she pulled out a pad of paper. "Okay, I take your names and dates of birth and then," she scribbled some figures, "I've got it. You'll be staying in lucky number seven." She enthusiastically thrust the key to number seven at them.

Once they were in the room and had turned the air conditioning on Mike blurted out, "What is this crazy shit?" Moses put his finger to his lips to silence Mike and led him to the bathroom. He turned on the shower and the tap and sitting on the toilet motioned to Mike that he should sit on the edge of the bath tub. He then leaned forward conspiratorially, his lips inches from Mike's ear.

"This place, this town, it's all run by Thomas Barker. You've heard of him haven't you?"

"Yes, Thomas Barker, he was a leader of some murderous sect. He wanted to start a war between the rich and the poor."

"That's right. He and his followers snuck into some mansions in the Hollywood hills and massacred the occupants. They left messages like 'rise outcasts' and 'kill the rich' on the walls in blood. They then went to skid row and shot dead some homeless people to make it look like the well to do were striking back."

"I read some things about it. They wanted to round up all the vagrants and put them in camps in the desert. Everybody in upscale neighborhoods started stocking up on guns and ammunition."

"That's right. It was a real panic for a while until they caught Barker. He was originally arrested on gun charges when the police pulled him over for driving under the influence of marijuana."

"Guns and grass, good combination."

"And I guess you heard about the trial?"

"Yeah it was a real circus."

"It also cost the state of California millions of dollars, but they were able to sentence Barker and some of his followers to death. Sentences that were later commuted to life in prison. He became a problem in prison. Some inmates wanted to kill him, while others became converts to his craziness. They sent him to a new prison conceived for difficult inmates that they had built here, in a town that used to be known as Petroville because of the abundance of oil that lay beneath its soil."

"So then what happened?"

"Freaks and psychos from across the nation flocked here to be close to the man they saw as their spiritual leader. All the normal people fled the area and the weirdos took over, putting their own people in charge of the city and county government."

"That explains our strange encounter with those crusty cops."

"You got it, they're in control and apply their philosophy of 'trashness' to everything."

"Trashness?"

"That's what they call it. 'You don't throw out the trash, the trash throws you out,' is their favorite slogan. They seem to be dedicated to clogging up the system so that it all breaks down."

"Well they've done a good job locally."

"Sure have, but I need to know if they want to expand and if our series of murders isn't part of their plan."

"So what are you going to do?"

"I'm going to go to the source. Tomorrow we're going to that penitentiary to talk with Thomas Barker."

"I've heard he's insane."

"Maybe he is, maybe it's all just an act. We'll see for ourselves."

"I've seen my limit of insanity for this month."

"You'll just have to find some reserve capacity within yourself." Moses turned off the gushing water and after finishing the beer and setting an alarm radio they lay down to sleep a slumber troubled by visions of chaos and destruction.

EIGHTEEN

Eight hours later they were awakened by the staid voice of the morning news drowned in a background of screeching static. It sounded like the announcement of the end of the world and Moses switched it off before it bored its way too deeply into their already fragile psyches. Resolutely they pulled on their clothes and tramped off to the motel's diner.

They were met at the door by the friendly familiar smell of breakfast being fried. The eatery was surprisingly clean and almost empty except for a pair of truckers in the back. Their waitress, who, though her head was shaved like the receptionist wore a neat uniform, took their order cheerfully and by the time they had finished their first cup of coffee slid scrumptious plates of bacon, sausage, eggs, and hash browns in front of them. They dug in, taking

128

sustenance from a pleasant breakfast in this oasis of normality and fortifying themselves to confront the curiousness that lay without.

There were more people on the streets of Barkersville than the day before. They also seemed to be going somewhere with a purpose rather than just drifting. Several times on the way to the prison Moses was forced to stop to let packs of locals with shaved heads and dressed in tatters cross in the middle of the street. Most of them wore Bowie knives on their belts, and some of them carried pump action shot guns.

They parked the car and walked to the entrance. The guards at the prison gates were obviously on edge. When Moses detailed the purpose of his visit, he was glared at as if he were responsible for the tension in the air. They passed through a series of barriers and control points that made them feel as if they were entering a citadel under siege.

After being led through a labyrinth of dark passages they found themselves in a conference room with a small middle aged man in prison clothes whose face was marked by years of incarceration. His hair was closely cropped and his beard was long. His eyes twinkled malignantly as if he held some terrible secret.

"So you boys come all the way up here to see me. Think I can help you with your problems?"

Moses sat down and looked across the table at the convict. "You remember me Mr. Barker?"

"Sure I remember you. I remember all my persecutors," he boomed in the voice of someone much larger. Then he chuckled and continued in a slightly less raucous tone, "Just kidding, you were just doing your job and me, I was just doing mine."

"Job huh? I was working for the LAPD. Who was your employer?"

"Me? I was a servitor, guided by the forces of nature to cleanse this world."

"Cleansing? You talked a lot about trash."

"The trash must be freed. We must open it all up. All the dumps. All the landfills. All the junkyards. All the prisons. All the mental hospitals. Let all the garbage that you try to hide away lie in the streets."

"And you're part of the garbage as well?"

"Yes that's right. They threw me out. I should stay out, lying naked in some public park with all my females."

"That's not something in my power to give you."

"I know that. Just want you to understand. I hear you're working as the personal cop of the rich and famous now."

"So you've been keeping tabs on me?"

"Can't know the game unless you know the players."

"And are you still one of the players?"

"You can see I'm on the sidelines for the moment."

"What about this town? What about your followers?"

"I've got nothing to do with that. I just put the idea out there, that trash shouldn't feel bad about being trash. Trash shouldn't feel bad about nothing. Because they are nothing. And knowing that will free them. The people on the top, the ones you protect, they don't care about following the rules. Just like us on the bottom, they're trash. Sometimes they need to be taken out." He pointed with his forefinger and cocked his thumb, "Bang, bang, bang, everybody's dead."

"So these recent killings. Your people have something to do with it?"

"My people? I don't have no people. Some fools want to think they belong to me and I belong to them. That's not my fault."

"Why don't you stop them? Tell them to go away?"

"You don't understand. I don't tell people what to do. They just do what they need to."

"What about this group that's killing celebrities now in LA?"

"Yes, they need to do it but it doesn't have anything to do with me. The middle is going away. When the middle goes away there won't be nothing left but the bottom and the top, and the bottom's not just going to stay on the bottom. They're going to stand up and then it's going to start."

"What's going to start?"

"Howdy Doody time."

"What's that?"

"When they're going to see the strings making them dance like puppets, and they're going to tear free."

"And where are you in all this?"

"Me, I'm just another symptom. I didn't make the disease and I'm not spreading it. If you think about it awhile you'll see it as it is. Society is war and war is society. We're all trying to destroy each other, but we don't want to know it."

"Damn, if I wanted philosophy I'd read it in a book instead of it getting second hand from someone who barely understood what they were reading."

"Yeah, that's right treat me like a fool. I've no interest in being some jail house philosopher or even any sort of philosopher at all. But there's nothing to do in here but think, so those thoughts go round and round in my brain till they come out. You shouldn't have asked for my opinion in the first place."

Moses sighed as though a mass of fatigue was weighing upon him. "We're sorry to have gotten you out of your cell for nothing."

Thomas' timeworn scowl turned into a gleeful grin and he chirped, "Never mind, never mind, always glad to have some visitors. Come back any time you feel lost." Then he sat there immobile, the smile frozen on his face as they got up and left, his eyes alone following their parting.

NINETEEN

For the first several hours of their trip back Mike remained silent, staring out at the bleak scenery passing by. It was only after they had passed the summit of the arid hills and began the descent towards Los Angeles that he spoke up, "I'm thankful to you for not firing me but why did you drag me along on this pointless trip?"

"Maybe it wasn't so pointless."

"How's that?"

"He might be involved."

"Barker? Why?"

"To put pressure on the parole board."

"But if they think he's still killing people they'll never let him out."

"Well, if he subtly intimates that it's the only way to get the carnage to stop they might be forced to."

"Hadn't thought of it from that angle."

"His idea, 'Howdy Doody time'. You know they teach that in German universities?"

"So they're Europeans. They like to dissect America as if it were a dead infected animal."

"Remember what he said, 'I'm just a symptom'?"

"Yeah, I guess I caught that, so?"

"So you know a disease by its symptoms. He and his followers were the original outbreak. Whoever's out there now killing my clients has got to have some link with them. And, though they may or may not be coconspirators, I felt going to see this man might somehow bring us closer to knowing."

"Just felt like a waste of time to me. Going to that freak show of a town."

"You see that's the thing. In that place the weirdos are in control. We're the strangers. We got a chance to study them up close and see what they're about. Whoever is committing these crimes is going to be like them, but they'll be hiding it. Now maybe we'll be able to see through them."

"Hey, whatever. I sure do feel that just being around those people did something to my mind, something bad."

"We can pick up some medication for you at a liquor store and then go to my place to get our heads straight."

"Sounds like the best plan you've had yet."

Forty minutes later Mike was sipping a whiskey cola that really hit the spot. The caffeine lifted him out of the languor that the mind bending journey to Barkersville had infused him with, and the alcohol calmed the nerves that had been badly frayed. He felt like he had been away for a long time, and that the world might have changed in his absence, so he turned on the evening news.

A freakishly over muscled man strode across the screen. His well-tanned skin made his blond hair and blue eyes seem even paler. With a different haircut and a uniform he'd be perfect for the part of a hero of the Afrikakorps marching out of the desert. The bleating voice of a television journalist introduced this singular personage. "Bavarian born California state senator and former action film star, Helmut Weissgruber, is now going to present his plan for saving the state's economy."

Arriving at a podium, he drew himself up imperiously behind it. "California is a power, a power that the world looks to," he proclaimed in a voice like that of a comedian lampooning the accent of a foreigner. "We must use our power to become what destiny ordains. Those that weaken us must be dealt with. I'm not just talking about welfare cheat parasites; we've already got a plan to force them to work. There is a more costly problem, all of these criminals lounging around in prison, playing checkers and watching TV, while we pay to clothe, feed, and house them. They should and they will be put to work as well."

He scanned the cameras that were transmitting his image, an otherworldly gleam in his eyes. "We will bring back the old ways of workhouses and chain gangs. These leeches will be made to pay their own way." The crowd before him applauded feverishly, and with a regal gesture he tilted his head up and gazed at the sky above him, brown with the exhaust of millions of good citizens on their way home from work.

Mike decided he didn't want to know what was going on in the world and turned off the TV. His fleeting feeling of well-being had passed. He blamed this Weissgruber. He didn't so much care about criminals. Whatever treatment they got was their problem. It was simply something about the paternalistic tone with which the Bavarian had set forth his proposal. Maybe it struck a chord for all the lost souls out there, but it didn't do anything for Mike. He knew that no one could help him find his way.

Moses noticed Mike's gloominess and, having watched the news broadcast from the corner of his eye while he fixed himself a drink, he divined its source. "That Helmut Weissgruber, he's another one peddling his own brand of BS. When you see how many people get taken in by it, you wonder what's wrong with the human race."

"Sounds like you've got some kind of issue with the man."

"I used to have him as a client. He treated everybody like dirt."

"But it must have been a contract that paid well. How did you lose it?"

"Let's just say we had ideological differences."

TWENTY

While Mike and Moses tried to chase the specters of the German giant and all his fellow megalomaniacs from their minds with alcohol, Weissgruber himself was riding in his limo puffing blithely on his pipe. He surveyed the throngs of people lining the sidewalks, tourists, peddlers, beggars, and the occasional whore, all were peons to him. "Wacht and dumm," he murmured, "wacht und dumm."

He felt triumphant and wished for an appropriate score to accompany him on his way home. He picked up the intercom's receiver and ordered the driver to put on his favorite music. Soon the strains of Wagner's Götterdämmerung resounded in the passenger compartment. It swirled together with the nicotine in his brain and he began to feel like some demigod rising towards a lofty dwelling.

Not wanting this diaphanous feeling to fade he called his butler and told him to put the same piece on his home stereo. As he stepped out of the limousine and walked towards the massive ornate door held dutifully open by his servant, the sound of the two out of sync recordings gave an impression that the horns were echoing off of distant hills. When he had broached the entrance of his vast manor the domestic bowed and slipped away. Helmut whistled and from the cavernous hallways a Rottweiler came running.

As Wagner Tubas lamented the death of Siegfried they made their way to the library. Weissgruber pulled down a book which caused the bookcase to swing inwards revealing a secret chamber. He stepped up to an altar above which hung a portrait of Hitler and lit candles that illuminated walls bedecked with Nazi paraphernalia. He knelt down and the robust canine sat beside him. "Mein Führer, ich diene ihnen und ich werde ihnen immer dienen."

He then stripped and began rolling playfully about with the dog on a deep plush carpet embossed with the flag of the Third Reich. He got on all fours and threw a come hither glance over his shoulder at his playmate. But instead of giving him the treatment he was longing for the Rottweiler bit ferociously into the skin of his back. Helmut turned over to defend himself from the attack but his bloated muscles were useless, serving only to provide more flesh for the merciless fangs to rip away.

At about three A.M. the butler rose from his bed in a small chamber hidden away in the depths of the mansion. He tiptoed through its broad hallways. Senator Weissgruber often smoked some marijuana before retiring and there was sometimes a half smoked joint or two to be found. He sniffed the air for traces of the sharp scent of cannabis and finding none he crept on.

When he got to the library he immediately sensed that there was something amiss. A smell like that of fresh meat hung in the air. Then he heard the sound of an animal panting. Had the dog gotten into one of the refrigerators? Then he saw the gap in the library shelves. Had there been some sort of burglary? He knew he should probably run away but overcome with curiosity he inched his way towards the opening.

He froze in place upon seeing the blood spattered Rottweiler lying on the national socialist carpet. The dog barked at him twice, not aggressively, but frolicsome, as if the domestic might have come to play with him. Leaning a bit nearer he caught sight of the former master of the house's torn body.

Cautiously he backed away. When he got to the hallway he began moving quicker, throwing fleeting glances over his shoulder to assure himself that the murderous animal wasn't following him. When he got to a phone he forced his shaking hand to dial 911. The operator had trouble believing what he told her. That a movie star politician was lying dead, killed by a Rottweiler, sounded a lot like the sort of drug filled fantasies and psychotic delusions she was accustomed to hearing at this time in the morning. Nevertheless, she was required to dispatch police and an ambulance.

TWENTY ONE

Lisa Stave got a call at about six o'clock in the morning. She wasn't given many details, just that another celebrity had died and that the circumstances of his death were far from ordinary. Her partner had already been called to the scene and after some hesitation she decided to call Moses while she was on the way. Moses decided to bring Mike along so, an hour later, the four of them were standing in front of the Weissgruber residence.

A squad of bored and tired police were standing facing a frantic hoard of journalists. One of them recognized Lisa and rushed over, followed by a camera crew, to interview her. "Is this another victim of the celebrity cult killers?"

"So you've come up with a name for them. I would think you could come up with something better."

"What are you calling them?"

"Writing headlines isn't our business. Catching criminals is."

"Well, what progress have you made?"

"Look, I'm working right now. Why don't you arrange an interview with the department's public relations. They'll answer your questions."

"I think the viewers would like to hear something from someone who's on the case, someone like you."

Lisa shook her head, "I've no comment to make at this time. Any information that I give might hinder the investigation."

The TV journalist was on the point of posing a more probing question when the body was wheeled out, and she rushed back to get some images of the bloody remains being carted away from the luxurious home. When they were free of observers and eavesdroppers Lisa, closely shadowed by detective Ruh, walked over to Moses.

"So another one of your clients gets it."

"He was an ex-client."

"Oh, why did he cancel your services?"

"Actually it was me who stopped working for him."

"Why?"

"I just didn't want to work for him anymore. I got a strange feeling around him. You know I'm used to odd individuals, but there was something about this guy. I couldn't stand being around him. I got the feeling that he was into some strange shit."

"Perhaps something like Nazism or bestiality?"

"What? Bestiality and Nazism?"

"Apparently he was residing in some special world where the two made a good mix. Still, we don't know why his guard dog went berserk and tore him to pieces."

"I know the service he retained after mine worked with dogs a lot. Me, I think they're unreliable. They scare off petty criminals but professionals find ways of controlling them."

"Then you might be able to be of help. Someone, maybe working for these 'celebrity cult killers', could have gotten to this dog and taken control of him. We're going to the kennel where it was kept right now. Care to come along?"

"I'm ready to do anything to clear this mess up."

Mike and Moses followed the unmarked police car across town to Silver Lake. The name must have been thought up by real estate developers to promote the place. There was no lake, only a reservoir surrounded by a barbwire topped fence. The kennel was across the street from a park adjacent to the open air cistern. It consisted of a cinder block building with two rows of chain link fence cages for the dogs.

Stepping out of their cars the four investigators were met with the plaintive howls of the imprisoned hounds. Pampered pups being walked by their masters in the nearby patch of green pricked up their ears at the sound of a suffering they'd never know. The kennel had the appearance of a business being run on the lowest possible budget and perhaps even with a few violations.

Detective Stave rang the buzzer beside the door and a bleary voice answered, "What? Who's that?"

"LAPD," she announced authoritatively.

"Did something happened? Why are you here?"

"Just let us in!"

"Okay, Okay," the voice from within stammered and after a few seconds a disheveled man in his late twenties opened the door. He appeared panicked at the sight of the four of them. "I didn't do anything; I just work here."

In a calmer tone Lisa said, "No one has accused you of anything we just want to talk."

He turned and led them to a sparsely furnished employee's break room. It had a refrigerator and a microwave oven, but it was so filthy and reeking of canine musk that they wondered how anyone could eat there. He sat down at a table and Lisa, Moses and Mike installed themselves facing him. Detective Ruh, as usual, hung back and observed.

Lisa began the questioning, "So what's your name, how long have you worked here, and what's your post?"

"Joe Rank, about five years, general manager."

"Why this job?"

"I used to love dogs."

"Used to?"

"I've gotten sick of them. Can't stand them anymore."

"What exactly sickens you about them?"

"They're dirty."

"You don't look so clean yourself."

"What's the point? When I come here to work every day."

"What about the clients? If they saw your appearance?"

"The clients don't come here. The boss makes sure of that."

"And the boss is?"

"Tony Mass."

"And what's his story."

"His story? I don't think he has one."

"What do you mean?"

"He doesn't come here often and never talks about himself. He just deals with the clients."

"And the clients don't know about the state of this place?"

"No, we drive the dog out to them and let it loose on their property."

"How do you make sure that the dog knows who it's supposed to protect and who it's supposed to attack?"

"We hold a training session in which the dog is familiarized with the people at the property they'll be guarding."

"Has a dog ever gone after somebody he shouldn't have?"

Joe gaped at Lisa with bugged out eyes, "No, that's never happened. Though we cut some corners here and there to keep costs down, our trainer knows what he's doing."

"You're sure about that?"

"Yeah, positive."

"We'll get back to this trainer. What about sex?"

Joe turned pale and began to tremble, "That, that girl I picked up downtown. She tricked me. I thought she was really a female and I didn't know she was going to ask me for money."

Lisa held back a chuckle, "We don't want to hear about any of your personal history. We want to know about the dogs and the clients."

Joe glanced about the room nervously, "Well, sometimes we get an animal who's acting a bit different. They'll get overly affectionate with anyone who gets near them. They'll like, you know, hump their leg."

"Lots of dogs do that."

"Yeah, but these dogs are trained. They're supposed to be cured of that."

"So if they do it anyway?"

"Probably means someone is using them for something kinky."

"And you just let that happen?"

"Well, the customer is king."

Officer Stave stepped towards the kennel manager aggressively and put her hands on her hips. "What the hell are you running here? Some kind of doggy brothel?"

Her partner stymied a laugh and the object of her wrath cringed. "My boss makes the rules. All I do is follow them. If we refused these customers then they'd simply go somewhere else."

Lisa continued in a menacing tone. "I don't know what kind of crime you can be charged with but I'm sure that we can find something." She looked at her partner and he nodded gravely. "We can perhaps charge you with conspiracy or complicity."

A panicked look contorted Joe's face, "conspiracy or complicity in what?"

"Murder. One of your dogs ripped Senator Weissgruber to shreds."

"Murder? But it's all just an accident. He was probably playing some freaky games with that Rottweiler and it went berserk and killed him."

"We have a good reason to believe that he was trained to attack this particular client."

"Trained to attack Weissgruber? Who would do that?"

"You've heard about this cult of celebrity stalkers?"

"Yes, what, you think they're connected?"

"Might very well be."

Joe looked sick and pale. "How did this happen to me? I do a simple job for a low wage. I don't deserve to be involved in something like this."

Seeing that he had been sufficiently softened up she decided to cajole him. "Maybe you don't but that doesn't mean that somebody else doesn't. That trainer, I'd like to know more about him."

"I've got his file in the office." He pointed towards a door behind him.

"Lead me to it." She then followed Joe closely (she knew that people in the state that he was in sometimes pulled a weapon out of somewhere and started shooting) to the adjacent room that had been made up into an office. She rested her hand on the butt of her automatic as he lifted the file out of a rusty cabinet. "Spread it out on the table."

He laid the pages out on the table. Lisa decided it would be better to have her partner with her to keep an eye on the still potential suspect while she looked them over. "Hey, Ruh, can you come in here?"

Detective Ruh entered the dingy room with watchful eyes. Joe leaned back against the wall and closed his eyes tightly as if trying to block out some horrible thought or memory. Lisa pushed the sheets of paper about with the tip of a pen till she found a resume that she then read from. "Robert Slack, dog handler for the US army stationed in Berlin. That's some qualification. What's he doing working in a dump like this?"

Joe started running his eyes over the floor as if he were following the meandering of a crazed cockroach. "Most people don't stay here so long so we don't ask too many questions about their work history or motivations."

"We might consider that criminal negligence." She glanced towards detective Ruh to solicit his opinion.

"We might very well at that."

Joe looked up at them his upper lip trembling, "I have to work with the personnel that's available."

Lisa squinted her eyes, "Why are you so nervous? You're making me nervous too."

"I've got a disorder, an anxiety disorder. That's why I work with animals and not people."

"So people make you nervous? You got some medication for that?"

"Yes, it was prescribed by the doctor."

"So take your meds and try to relax."

Joe pulled a pill bottle out of his pocket and poured out a handful.

"Take just one. We don't want to have to bring you to the hospital."

Sheepishly, he took one and put the rest away.

Lisa read the address at the top of the resume. "85 Echo park boulevard. He still live there?"

"That's where his paychecks go."

"When did you last see him?"

"Three days ago, he called in sick. I just thought of something else. He took this Rottweiler home with him. He said it was for some special training, detecting weapons and explosives."

"And you just let him take the dog out of here?"

The tranquilizer appeared to be taking effect and Joe answered mistily, "He was supposed to be an expert."

Lisa turned to consult her partner, "Maybe we should get over there?"

"Maybe we should." He pointed at the kennel manager. "What about him?"

She threw a depreciative look at Joe. "Leave him, I don't think he's capable of much."

TWENTY TWO

At the wheel of the bulky LTD, Moses had trouble keeping up with the sleeker, recent model Chevy Caprice. The police detectives also had a flashing red and blue dash deck light that helped open holes in traffic. Holes that were closing right when Moses tried to pass through them. Mike, however, was grateful that his non-stop cursing obviated the need for conversation. Anything that would help to avoid having to talk about the perverse recent developments in the case was welcome.

The advantages that their adversaries had over them were becoming more and more obvious. They were completely hidden; there was no knowing who might be working for them. They had no limits, morally or otherwise. They were capable of any sort of atrocity and had no qualms about injuring or even

150

killing anyone. But most of all they seemed fanatically dedicated to their warped mission, to the point of being ready to sacrifice their own lives.

When they arrived at 85 Echo Park Boulevard, Stave and Ruh once again took advantage of their status as official law enforcement officers and double parked right in front of it. Moses was forced to drive down the block to find a space to accommodate his ride. By the time he and Mike had made their way back the detectives were deep in consultation in the shade of a tree. Something seemed to be troubling them as they examined the facade of the white stucco apartment house.

They turned to Mike as he approached. "What do you think of it?" Lisa asked.

"It's definitely not luxurious but I've seen worse."

She gruffly exhaled with exasperation. "I'm not asking for architectural criticism. I want to know if it's safe."

"Safe?"

"Yeah, this guy was in the military. He might know something about booby traps. He might have left a surprise for us."

When Mike realized that his advice was being sought on an important matter, a good part of his feeling of helplessness was lifted from him. The idea that two LAPD veterans needed his input did a lot for his self-confidence, so he answered with as much authority as he could muster, "We'd call in the bomb disposal squad if we had time."

"What if you had to get into some place right away?"

"Then we didn't always follow official procedure," Mike chortled.

"Hey, you can tell me. I can keep a secret." Lisa inveigled.

"Say we needed to crawl into some place that looked unsavory. What we would do is toss in a few grenades to hopefully set off whatever might be waiting for us."

"Well we don't have any grenades." She looked about her and spied a row of stones bordering a flower beds. She tilted her head towards them. "One of them might have enough impact."

Mike walked over and picked up a hefty piece of granite. "This might do the trick."

"What are you waiting for? Robert Slack lived on the ground floor left."

"You people need to get back," Mike stated bluntly and, when the three of them had taken shelter behind the Chevy, he placed himself about ten feet in front of the apartment's window. Exhilaration filled him as he poised himself to throw. He felt like he had when he was back in the field and, after months of searching, they'd finally acquired a target. He launched the projectile and threw himself to the ground. When it struck the window an explosion was almost simultaneously set off, and he was showered with broken glass.

Seconds later an unwashed pudgy man in shorts and a sleeveless t-shirt came running out of the neighboring apartment. "What are you people doing?" he shouted gesticulating frantically. He then pointed at Mike who was still on the ground. "I saw you throw that rock."

"Yes, I threw the rock," Mike admitted. "And it exploded," he added pointedly.

The man looked flustered, "These rocks, they don't explode. You did something to them, I'm going to press charges."

Lisa intervened while Moses and detective Ruh hung back. "Detective Stave, LAPD," she introduced herself while pulling back her jacket to reveal the gun and badge on her belt, "of course you can press charges if you want but did you know that the tenant of this apartment was a terrorist."

"A terrorist? I thought he was a dog handler."

"That was just his day job. Did you know that harboring a terrorist is a serious crime?"

"Harboring! A crime! I just rented him an apartment."

"Maybe you should just go back inside and take a nap and maybe a shower."

Flummoxed, the apartment manager turned and picked his way through the wreckage left by the explosion back to the door of the damaged building. Mike looked at detective Stave and realized that he had been played. All the confidence that he had felt faded away.

"Thanks," Lisa quipped mockingly, "now we don't need a warrant. This explosion is more than enough for probable cause."

"Yeah, I'm happy to be a fool for you."

"Everybody is," detective Ruh interjected.

A hard look came over Mike's face. "Don't expect any more help from me."

"Come on, be a sport. This is the big leagues here. The game can get rough. You can't take it hard. We'll squash any charges that are brought against you."

"If that bomb had been more powerful it might have done me some damage."

"But you can relax now. We'll get the bomb squad to clear the place and then we'll go in."

After the experts had come and found the other surprises that Robert Slack had left, a trip wire attached to a double barrel shot gun and a vat rigged to pour acid over whoever came through the door, the four of them entered the diabolical dog handler's den. Except for a mattress on the floor and a TV on a stand with some drawers, there was no sign that someone had lived there. There was a suit of armor of the sort used for training attack dogs along with a collection of whips, chains, and electroshock devices hanging on the wall.

They all stood there taking in the oddness of the place. It looked more like a sinister torture chamber than a domicile. Finally their eyes came to rest upon a male mannequin on all fours in the middle of the room. Moses bent over to examine it more closely. It had a padded surface that felt like human flesh and an opening between the buttocks. For some reason it was wearing a leather motorcycle jacket. He scrunched up his face, "What the hell is this thing?"

Nobody dared venturing a guess except for Mike, "Maybe it's one of those new sex dolls."

"What the fuck?" Moses blurted out.

"Yeah, I think I saw something about that on internet."

"What kind of freaky internet sites do you visit?"

Mike blushed slightly and stammered, "I use the internet in the back of a liquor store; they always have lots of sleazy stuff popping up because of other users."

"Are you sure about that? If you got some tendencies that we should know about we're going to find out."

"No, I'm normal. I mean, relatively, compared to a lot of people lurking on the web."

"Hey okay, I guess everybody needs their secret place," Moses jeered.

Lisa threw him an irritated glance, "This is serious business. The more deviant our perpetrators are the more dangerous they stand to be. It's beginning to seem as though they are so estranged from humanity that people are just objects, pieces in a game they are playing, and killing them has no more meaning than breaking a cheap vase."

"Okay, sorry I just thought that some levity might lighten things up."

"The important thing is finding out what went on here."

She went to the television stand and pulled one of the drawers open. She took out a spray can. At first she thought it might be mace or pepper spray but then she read the label, "Whiff-a-stiff?"

She sprayed some of it into the air and sniffed it. "Ugh," she coughed and read the rest of the label, "He'll hump you like you were a real bitch!"

A trace of the odor reached detective Ruh and he wrinkled his nostrils in disgust. "That's worse than a week dead body."

Stave looked through some other drawers and found a camera, a collapsible tripod, and some cassettes. She looked through them till she found one labeled, "Weissgruber-Rottweiler." After turning on the television and connecting the camera she began playing it.

Robert Slack appeared in the dog trainer armor. The Rottweiler jumped on him, biting and wrestling him to the ground. She fast forwarded. The dog was seen humping the human mannequin, when it finished the handler rewarded him with a doggy treat. She fast forwarded again. The dog was seen going at the sex doll once more, and the handler was again in the armor. When the dog got done with his business it was shocked repeatedly and attacked his tormentor who stood his ground.

After almost at minute of torture the dog turned its wrath upon the mannequin. The handler let it give the human substitute a thrashing that would kill a normal person before pulling it off and rewarding it with a doggy treat. The video ended with the dog munching contentedly, seeming no more menacing than any household pet.

A heavy silence hung over the room. No one seemed to want to venture a commentary on such an edifying spectacle. After a moment that felt much longer than it actually was Moses spoke up, "Well now we know that they are ready to get recruits wherever they can, even the animal kingdom." The others gave him a look of puzzlement mixed with distaste; how could he make light of something so revolting? He shrugged, "We've got to face what we're dealing with here. These people might as well be some evil race from another planet. And we, we're like some kind of space explorers."

Lisa threw him a droll glance, "I don't think this is something to make light of."

"Me neither, we've got to get to whoever is responsible for all of this."

Lisa's eyes roved about the apartment. "We need to search this place. This being official police business the two of you will have to wait outside." Complacently, Mike and Moses left the scene and went to wait on the lawn in front of the building. They stood around for a while feeling useless until Moses happened to set his eyes on some garbage cans alongside the apartment building.

He pointed it out to Mike. "We're going to stop wasting our time and get into this investigation." They poured the contents, which consisted mostly of fast food packages and beer bottles, out on the ground and started sorting through it. The fetid smells of the tenants' unhealthy diets made them feel a bit like they were performing an autopsy. After digging through the trash for a dozen minutes, Mike came upon something looking like a fanzine but its front page didn't feature any punk or indie bands.

"Maps to the Stars' Homes and How to Kill Them", it read.

He showed it to Moses who began to examine its pages. They had been stained by beer but were still legible. Mike looked over his shoulder at the discovery. It contained not only directions to the homes of the rich and famous but their schedules and favorite haunts. Even details of the security services that were supposed to protect them were revealed. Most ominously, it contained ads for gun shops and shooting ranges so would be stalkers might know where to arm themselves and hone their marksmanship.

As the curse that had been dogging them from the start would have it, there was no header identifying the author of this psychopathic publication. They tore through the pages without finding a single clue to its origins. It could have been made on any small offset printer and stapled together. The only lead was the ads. Whoever paid for them had to have had some contact with the person responsible. The closest address was "Gun Country" on Palm Boulevard in Burbank, so without any good-by to the pair of detectives who were still going over the apartment they headed north.

TWENTY THREE

Palm Boulevard was lined with the glittering facades of buildings housing motion picture related industries. By simply driving along it one could begin to feel as if they had been transported into the magic world of movies and a happy ending was waiting just ahead for them. Moses parked in a multilevel garage full of luxury cars. He and Mike rode a gleaming elevator down to street level and they emerged to a sidewalk along which strolled confident well-dressed Californians. None of them seemed at all alarmed by the muffled sound of gunfire. That the salvos came from actual weapons was evident from the singular cadence that both movies and fireworks couldn't duplicate. Every detonation was followed by the ping of a projectile striking a target.

The two of them knew that the noise was not that of a real firefight but, still shaken by their recent encounters with armed maniacs, they advanced towards the racket with trepidation. The by-passers sensed the lack of assurance in the pair and nudged them aside, as if they were some useless vagabonds blocking the way of people who had important business to do. Mike felt himself wishing that some crazed shooter would appear blasting everything that moved and that, after first crouching in shock, the good citizens would flee screaming in panic.

The timbre of the din changed as they entered the shop. A hollow echo was added to its tonality which made it seem more contained and less threatening. The evenly spaced reports were obviously coming from an indoor shooting range and bore no resemblance to the staccato bursts of a battle. The guns filling the cabinets lining the walls were also reassuring. If Armageddon was to start at least they'd be equipped to deal with it.

A fat and jovial looking man wearing a camouflage hunting cap and a shooting vest called out to them from behind the counter. "You boys looking for something?"

Moses wound his way through the array of armament to him. "Yes, I wanted to ask you some questions."

His grin turned into a scowl. "Oh goddamn, what are you? The police? The ATF?"

"No, I'm Moses Murphy the director of Hollywood Detectives."

"What the hell do you want with me?"

Moses pulled the beer stained zine out of his pocket and showed it to him. "You know what this is about?"

The man lost control of himself, "That motherfucking, 'Maps to the Stars' Homes and How to Kill them' has caused me so much goddamn trouble."

"Perhaps we can help."

"Can you get them to stop using the name of my business?"

"You didn't place an ad with them?"

"No, I never wanted anything to do with those people."

Moses turned to the page featuring the man's gun shop, "But this is an advertisement for this place no?"

"You've got to understand those people are crazy. They're like some kind of cult."

"A cult? That's exactly what we're looking for."

"I tried to find out about these weirdos myself. I didn't get too far. I found some of them selling this rag on Hollywood boulevard. I threatened to take some action against them but they got real aggressive with me. They said that they had powers and they could destroy me. A few days later I found something spooky on my doorstep, a decapitated pigeon wrapped in a movie trade magazine. After that some bad things started to happen to me so I stayed away from those people."

"What sort of bad things?"

The gun shop owner shivered and turned away. "I can't talk about that, I'm too frightened."

"Frightened? A big man like you? Look at all the guns you have."

"This is something you can't stop with a bullet unless...."

"Unless what?"

He stuck his index finger to his cap. "Unless you put the bullet in your brain and even then it might be waiting for you on the other side."

Mike gazed upon the man with stupefaction. What could have reduced a carefree weapons dealer to a state of childlike terror? It had the mark of the group they were after. He thought about resigning but he left the gun store owner there, staring up towards heaven with his finger stuck to the side of his head, and followed Moses back to the LTD.

TWENTY FOUR

Evening rush hour had arrived and the intrepid pair of private dicks drove southwestward against the home bound flow of commuters. Mike envied them in spite of the torturous hours stuck in traffic that they had yet to endure. At least they had a clear idea of where they were going. They weren't trapped in a struggle with an adversary who, in addition to all their other weaponry, had now added voodoo to their arsenal.

They were slowed to a crawl when they got to Hollywood boulevard. A flock of fools come from other neighborhoods, the suburbs, and even other states were cruising along hanging out the windows of their cars bobbing their heads and waving their arms desperately trying to attract some attention to themselves. Watching them act out their pathetic fantasies of being somebody unique in some special

163

place, Mike could almost identify with the people they were after.

It was all so ugly. Would it be so bad if something came along to wipe it all away? A tsunami of blood and flames come to rid the world of it. He watched the people roaming along the sidewalk. Most of them were dressed for a part in some movie that was playing in their heads. Perhaps the scenarist could rewrite their part so that it came to a sudden tragic end.

A couple blocks after Vine Street a man dressed all in black with a skull mask on was holding a sign up for passengers of passing cars to see. "Maps to the Stars' Homes and How to Kill Them 5.00$", it boldly declared. Mike poked Moses' shoulder and then pointed out the macabre figure. Moses nodded his head in acknowledgment and turned in to a parking lot that just happened to have a space available facing the horrific street vendor.

Passersby mostly jeered the spooky apparition and sometimes even threw trash at him. Now and then someone actually stopped and bought a copy of his lurid zine that he pulled out of a newspaper boy's bag he wore over his shoulder. After several hours had passed and he'd accumulated a decent sum of money, a pair of druggie street people approached and began harassing him. From the look of things they were trying to extort some of his earnings.

He had set his bag and sign down with seeming compliance and appeared to be on the point of handing over some of his hard earned cash when suddenly he lashed out with a combination of punches which knocked the would be shake down artists to the ground. They staggered away while looking back, shaking their fists and mouthing what Mike and Moses surmised were threats though they couldn't hear them, ensconced as they were in the LTD.

The merchant of the murderous publication pulled out his phone and made a call. Was it to report the incident? To whom? Several minutes after the call his persecutors were back armed with two by fours, probably pulled from a nearby construction site, and intent upon giving their defiant victim a serious beat down. Suddenly, a black van pulled up and a half dozen individuals all in the same black costume and death mask surged forth from it. They had their right hands cupped as if they might be holding weapons. The cowed thugs backed away to go in search of less forbidding prey.

When the band of grim reapers had climbed back in the van, Moses started his car's motor. The driver tried slipping away but was blocked by a pickup full of rednecks who had stopped to shout insults and threats at a bunch of goths gathered in front of a night club. Moses was able to pull up to one car length behind him.

He then followed the vehicle as it turned right towards the slightly more fluid traffic of Sunset Boulevard. After a few blocks it dropped off the gang of frightful enforcers in front of what looked like an abandoned house and they slunk inside. It then turned right on Vermont and drove on for a few blocks, until it came to a stop in front of a disused printing shop. The van pulled into the parking lot and the driver, who wore a red hooded sweat jacket, got out and went into the building.

Moses parked in front of the driveway of a garage that was closed for the night. He and Mike were able to see the lights come on inside the place. Through the glass brick windows of the cinder block structure the shadows of figures moving about in the interior could be made out. Something was going on in there, but they had no way of finding out what it was.

"Maybe we should call in the real police," Mike suggested.

"Call them for what?" Moses rebuked. "All we can see is some shop open at night. That's no sign of criminal activity."

"What about that vendor and the gang that came to protect him?"

"I admit that that's pretty strange, but not necessarily an arrestable offense."

"Maybe I could get a better look at what's going on in there."

"How's that?"

"Apply for a job."

"What?"

"I'll ring the doorbell and say I want to work for them."

"In the middle of the night?"

"I'll make myself look like some kind of bum. The kind of person who doesn't really know what they're doing and might show up anywhere at anytime asking for anything."

"You think you can be convincing?"

"Of course, because I don't know what I'm doing. I'm as completely lost as any derelict ambling about."

"But you're too clean."

"That can be fixed."

Mike switched off the indoor lights of the car and then slipped out, crouching low so as to be out of sight of anyone who might be keeping watch from the shop. He found a patch of dirt that used to be a lawn and began rolling about in it like a dog and rubbing the soil into his hair and onto his face. He soon looked like he had been sleeping in weed filled vacant lots for months.

Moses could barely make him out in the dim light of vandalized street lamps. "I'm impressed! Where did you pick that up?"

"In the service. They call it improvised field camouflage."

"Well, duty calls."

Mike ran to the end of the block doubled over behind the parked cars then came walking back on the printing shop's side of the street so it would look like he was coming from a downtown homeless shelter. He walked into the light issuing from the shop and pushed a buzzer beside the door. From the interior of the LTD Moses saw him be welcomed inside.

Moses had been maintaining surveillance on the printing shop for about ten minutes when it suddenly went dark. After a few minutes a reddish glow like that of something burning shone forth feebly from within. Moses decided he'd better investigate.

He left the car and made his way as stealthily as possible to the rear of the building. There, he found a stack of wooden pallets that he was able to climb up on. He tread cautiously across the gravel covered roof towards a skylight and peeked inside. Mike was stripped to the waist, gagged, and tied to a support column. Blood dripped from his head. Sinister statues resembling the idols of some pagan creed stood behind him shimmering in the crimson glow of the fires. Three men in tattered clothing were kneeling in a semi-circle facing Mike, their heads bowed as if they were praying. The driver of the van, his head still hidden by his sweat jacket's hood, stood next to Mike his arms raised above his head.

Moses pulled his portable phone out and selected Lisa Stave's number. It rang for a minute before the voice mail came on. He fumbled in his wallet till he found detective Ruh's card and dialed his number. A panicked voice answered immediately. "So you heard about it! It happened just after you left."

"What happened? I'm here at 1226 north Vermont and..."

Detective Ruh cut Moses short. "I don't care where you are. I've got much bigger problems."

"What problems?"

"Lisa has been shot."

"When's that?'"

"Three hours ago. We were coming out of that apartment we investigated today and just when she got to the car she fell to the ground. We didn't hear the shot or see the shooter. Must have been a sniper. She's in intensive care."

"That's horrible news, but I've got a serious situation here myself."

"Hey, you're just going to have to deal with whatever trouble you've gotten yourselves into on your own."

"I think I've found them."

The tone of Ruh's voice changed suddenly from dismissive to interested, "Them? You mean the people responsible for all of this?"

"Yeah, I'm at 1226 north Vermont. They've got Mike tied up."

"How did he get himself tied up?"

"It's complicated. You just better get someone down here soon. It looks like he might be in danger."

Moses put his phone away and looked down into the atelier. A wavering orange light which made seeing through the wired glass difficult had filled the interior. He found a spot in the skylight where the glass had been replaced with a sheet of plastic. He cautiously peeled it away. Through the opening he had a clear view of curious happenings inside.

Mike was still tied up unconscious and the men in rags were kneeling where they had been, but they were bathed in the light of flames coming from fires set in steel barrels. The lips of the man standing beside Mike protruded from the shadow of his hood and were moving as if he were repeatedly kissing the air and a faint chanting in some unintelligible language could be heard. But the most disturbing development was the appearance of a knife in the raised fist of the master of the weird ceremony.

He lay his left hand upon Mike's head and the ritual's sacrifice instantly awoke, struggling against his bonds. Moses slipped out his automatic. He didn't have a clear shot at the high priest of the unholy rite, but he spied a stack of paper that might cushion a fall under another skylight. He ran across the roof and, after kicking a hole in it large enough for him to pass through, he leaped down into the midst of the killer cult. As he fell the knife plunged towards Mike's chest and his head slumped to his chest.

Moses drew back to a corner where he had all of them in his sight. He ordered them to lie down on the ground but their leader protested. "But, you don't understand; this isn't what you think," he screeched in a strangled sounding brogue.

Moses pointed his gun at the man's head while still watching over the supine forms in front of him through his peripheral vision. "Not what I think? You just massacred someone. Put that knife down."

The man dropped the knife and then with his hands raised before him crept towards Moses. "I've come here to this country to make things right, to make things as they were meant to be," he continued in his spooky almost hysterical accent.

"Stay the fuck away from me or I'll make you the way you were meant to be, good and dead."

In spite of Moses' threats the man kept coming and he was about to open fire when a loud pounding was heard at the shop's door. It burst inward and a pack of police swarmed in flinging the blood spattered cult leader to the ground. Detective Ruh entered the scene and began ordering the uniformed officers about. The fires were put out, the suspects all handcuffed, and Mike was cut free. From the location of the wound and the profusion of blood they assumed he was dead.

Ruh walked over to check out Mike's body. He felt a strong pulse at the victim's neck and the paramedics were quickly called in. They hesitated a moment before the terrible stare of the idols, then bent down to try and revive their offering and found that he wasn't wounded, only unconscious. The sacrifice's performer lay handcuffed on the ground, none of the police willing to risk soiling their uniforms with blood by helping him to his feet. He kept mumbling to himself as his acolytes were led away.

Ruh put on a pair of latex gloves and picked up the knife that had been used in the ritual. He looked it over for several seconds and then walked over to a table and laid it down for closer examination. He soon discovered that it was no normal knife at all. When its point stabbed something, the blade retracted into the handle making it impossible to wound anyone with it. The movement of the blade actuated a pump that squirted a red liquid resembling blood. The most surprising feature of all was a hypodermic syringe that sprang out at the point of the blades most rearward travel to inject the human sacrifice with drugs.

Ruh pushed the man on the floor up into a seated position with his foot and then squatted down to look him in the eyes. He held the contraption resembling a knife out so that the detainee could see it. "What's this? And who are you?"

"It's nothing that important and my name is Bryan Mcbrade," the man answered in a wavering brogue.

The detective waved the device around indicating the print shop cum pagan temple. "And all of this set up here? What is that?"

"It's a business. I'm a businessman."

"Businessman? What the hell kind of business you in?"

"Why, printing obviously."

A Moses brought a copy of "Maps to the Stars' Homes and How to Kill them" over to Ruh. The detective glanced through its pages with a look of displeasure on his face. "So this is the rag you're selling?"

"Not me personally but the people working for me."

"You mean that brainless garbage that we took out of here?"

"Why, yes but they're not really garbage, just people who are lost in this confusing world."

"And so I guess you're the one to show them the way right?"

"I simply provide a place for them. A role to play in the great drama of Hollywood."

"So have you heard about this group of celebrity stalkers? Seems that they have some cult like tendencies, just like your own little group."

The man turned away, fake blood dripped from his forehead and his cheeks were stained black from the grime of the shop floor. "Of course I've heard of them. Almost everyone has."

Detective Ruh ran his eyes over the besmirched surface of the suspect's face. In spite of his powerless posture a glimmer of undimmed confidence shone in his eyes. "So what's with this theater here? Why were you pretending to sacrifice this man?"

"It's something that my people need. It helps them to feel as if they belong to something, something stronger than themselves."

"They're your people? Like your property or your slaves or something?"

"They've come to me and I use them."

"Use them for what?"

"Why for making money of course."

"But, they're not your employees?"

"They sell my publication and I give them a place to sleep and food to eat."

"Sounds like slavery to me."

"Lots of people have the homeless selling newspapers for them."

"But those are public service journals, not sheets encouraging people to murder."

"I don't encourage anyone to do anything I just help show the way to those that might be so inclined."

"Oh, so you're just an ordinary citizen trying to help make the world a better place?"

"You might say that."

"What about the other sacrifices you performed? What did you do with them afterwards?"

"I let them sleep off the effects of the drug and then I drove them downtown and let them go with some money for breakfast and a bottle."

"You just let them go, even though they knew that your little ceremony here was hoax and no one actually was killed? Weren't you afraid they'd let your band of followers know you were a fake?"

"I strongly admonished them not to come back. They were usually terrified. They are very superstitious. Most people who live rough chaotic lives are. They feel that some awful fate has them in its grasp."

"You seem to present your case pretty well."

"I'm not guilty of anything that's all. I'm simply filling a certain void."

"Void huh, how'd you come up with this idea?"

"I've always been interested in ancient beliefs, especially those having to do with the Gods of death. It seems that the older the pantheon the more prominent that the God of death is in it. I came to Los Angeles after several years spent as a stage actor and playwright in Dublin and London. I thought that there would be a place for me here."

"You should know before your go," Ruh quipped, "LA's full up of strango eurotrash."

Immune to mockery Mcbrade continued, "The only position I could find for myself was selling maps to the stars' homes on Hollywood boulevard. It was not very rewarding work and I was often chased off by bands of thugs selling similar products. Once they robbed and beat me so badly that I spent some time in the hospital. While I was lying on my hospital bed on morphine a reportage about celebrity stalkers came on the telly. As I watched it the idea came upon me. I'd create my own band of map sellers more fearsome than those that had beaten me. We would be united in a dreadful faith, the worship of the ancient Gods of the dead. We ourselves would pose as dealers of death distributing guides to aspiring murderers."

"So you admit you're aiding potential killers?"

"I said it was simply a pose. I imagine that most people buy my publication for its novelty value, nothing more than a grotesque souvenir."

"Don't you think it's a little bit curious that both you and this murky organization go into business at about the same time in about the same way?"

"We're really not alike at all. They seem to be bent upon sowing terror, while I'm mostly interest in reaping financial benefits."

"You may have different goals but you seem to be sending out the same message, it's time to kill the rich and famous, and you both seem to be spreading the word with devotees that appear to be brainwashed."

"As far as us being alike I would put that down to concurrent consciousness."

"Concurrent consciousness? What the hell is that?"

"It's a theory of the sociologist John Underway. It postulates that in times of uncertainty many groups will emerge, each of them bearing similar characteristics. This is because their adherents and leaders are all the products of the same dysfunctional institutions."

"Yeah, but you're a foreigner. Wouldn't dysfunctional institutions in your own country be to blame for whatever is out of whack in your mind?"

"Hollywood is an international institution. It twists people up everywhere so that they will fit into its molds."

"So you feel that they have done you wrong and now they owe you something back? That's about the same philosophy of every low-life I've ever arrested."

"I'm no common criminal. The work that I'm doing is special. It is helping to bring into being another world."

"Damn, that sounds like the thinking of a crazed suicide sect leader. Anyway, it's not my problem. I just decide what to charge vermin like you with. I don't psychoanalyze you."

The Mcbrade strained futilely against the cuffs on his wrists. "Charge me with what? I've committed no crime."

"Oh, what are you, a lawyer? We can always find something to pin on people who are a problem for us. For starters you lit a fire in this place, maybe we can get you for arson. And then there are these people you've got working for you. There're obviously suffering from different sorts of mental incapacity. Exploiting their disability for financial gain is probably illegal as well."

The accused man lifted up his head to reveal a face infused with arrogant self-righteousness. "So, like some small town cop you're going to fabricate a pretext to take me in?"

"Fabricate? I don't have to fabricate anything. You're not clean. In fact you're dirtier than a dive bar's toilet. You do stuff that hurts people or may lead to people being hurt. As far as what laws have been broken, like I said that's for the courts to decide."

"I'm sure that at least one juror will see the righteousness of my crusade."

"Righteousness? Crusade? Are you trying for an insanity defense? Here's something you need to understand; we don't have to prove a connection between you and this gang of celebrity stalkers. All we have to do is let the jury make the connection. What's more we don't have to convict you of anything. We can simply find a way to deport you."

The defiant look softened and his eyes appeared to plead. "No please don't send me back."

"You're going to have to give me a reason. I don't care about helping you. I need to stop these murders."

Everyone stood silently watching the now humbled figure. Mike and Moses were surprised and impressed by the aggressive interrogation that the formerly reticent detective Ruh had carried out.

They both put it down to the shooting of Lisa Stave and wondered how badly she was actually injured. Ruh stood up and gazed down his nose with cold indifference at his detainee.

After a minute of reflection the beaten man decided to acquiesce to his accuser's demands. "I've been in contact with them."

Ruh pulled out a pen and pad of paper. "Been in contact with them? How?"

"They're truly insane these people. Compared to them everything I'm doing is a sad joke."

"Oh, so they're serious? More serious than your righteous self? What did they have to say to you?"

"They said that I was a heretic and that I had to pay."

"Pay? How?"

"In cash, fifty thousand dollars."

"You have that much money?"

"I have thirty people selling this magazine. They each sell about twenty a day at five dollars each. So I gross about three thousand."

"Hot damn! I should start my own cult," Ruh jested. The cops, who were standing around following the interrogation to see if it might give them some pointers should they ever become detectives themselves, shared in the merriment and chuckled derisively at the expense of their cowering captive.

"So," Ruh went on with a graver voice, "the killers wanted some of your money."

"Yes, and when I didn't pay some of the people working for me disappeared."

"I guess you didn't want to call the police did you?"

"Street people disappear all the time don't they?"

"But you knew they hadn't simply disappeared?"

"There were rumors. Everyone was talking about some new organization that was going to take everything over. A group that even the most dangerous thugs were afraid of."

"So what were you going to do?"

"I was going to pay."

"When?"

"It hadn't been arranged yet."

Ruh smiled a broad triumphant smile and pointed his trigger finger at Mcbrade jabbing it towards him to punctuate his words. "You're going to tell them you got the money and arrange a payoff, and we're going to be there to catch these bastards."

"I can't do that," the recalcitrant informer sniveled, "I'll be dead, these people are mad, dangerous."

Ruh brought his menacing finger closer to Mcbrade's face, almost poking him in the eye, "You'll do what I tell you if you want out of the mess you're in."

"I'll do as you say, but my death will be on your conscience."

"Nobody's going to die as long as you follow my orders, and anyway I don't have a conscience when it comes to dealing with the likes of you. You got a contact number for these people?"

"Yes, it's on my cell phone."

The officers that had searched and cuffed him stood him up and, after freeing his hands, gave him his phone.

"Put the loud speaker on," Ruh advised sternly.

Mcbrade complied and then dialed the number. All present bent forward to hear the voice of the killer cult's mysterious master.

"So Bryan my friend," an electronically scrambled voice answered, "you've decided to come around to my way of thinking."

"Yes, I have the money. Where do you want me to bring it?"

"It's not for me to want but for you," the voice continued with a menacing tone that somehow slithered through the circuits of the scrambling device, "the money itself isn't important; fealty is. You must acknowledge that I am the lord of big name death and any proceeds gained from it are mine."

"You said fifty thousand dollars."

"That's right. I won't take everything from you. I appreciate your work and want you to stay in business."

The load of terror that had been weighing on Mcbrade was lifted. "How should I get your payment to you?"

"I'll tell you shortly but first I want to be sure that the detectives are listening closely."

The face of Mcbrade was anew seized by fear, "Detectives? I'm all alone here."

"Oh, don't lie to me Bryan. I know exactly where you are and who you are with. But I don't mind. In fact it's what I planned. I want them to come with you."

"You want me to bring the police with me?"

"No, I want the watchdogs of the stars, Mike Johnson and Moses Murphy to tag along."

Moses grabbed the cell phone out of Mcbrade's hand, "What if we don't want to be guests at whatever party you're planning?"

A distorted chuckle buzzed through the scrambler and the voice ordained, "You shall be there, you shall be. If you aren't then your business won't last another week."

"You want me to believe that you'll stop your campaign of murder if I go where you tell me?"

"I'm not promising that, just assuring that it'll all be over for you in this town if you don't cooperate."

"Alright, fine, where are we supposed to go?"

"Be at Union Station tomorrow at nine o'clock, bring the money and the phone you're talking on now, only Mcbrade, you, and Johnson. If anybody else shows up there's going to be trouble."

"Don't worry, we'll come alone."

"Till tomorrow mister rent a cop."

Moses lifted the phone high over his head as if he were going to dash it to pieces on the floor but then relaxed and put it away in his pocket.

Ruh observed him clinically, "Are you going to be there?"

"Yes of course."

"But these people. You've seen what they do. They're merciless."

"Well I'm fine with that. I wouldn't want these bastards to have any mercy for me and I don't plan on showing any to them." He patted the nine millimeter under his jacket. "I just want a chance to get close to them."

"Okay then, I'll leave you to it."

TWENTY FIVE

The next morning the trio passed through the doors of Union Station into the opulent interior that lay waiting to welcome the world to the exotic realm of Los Angeles. They seated themselves in the luxuriantly spacious easy chairs to await the call of the self-proclaimed lord of big name death. A tour group of elderly folks that had just arrived by train from the heartland gazed about themselves awestruck as if they were pilgrims at the Vatican.

After sitting there for a while, they began to think they were being left off the hook by their deranged tormentor. Perhaps he had decided to take up something like burning ants to death with a magnifying glass and leave them alone. To alleviate the tedium Mcbrade pulled out a flask and took a generous swig. Sadly, his generosity didn't extend to Mike and Moses, and he offered none to them.

They began eyeing the tables of the Station's bar set up across from them, cordoned off from foot traffic by a velvet rope. They looked at each other and wordlessly came to the conclusion that they'd rather be on the other side of that rope sipping a cocktail.

They were on the point of getting up and walking over to the terrace when the phone Moses had confiscated from Mcbrade rang. With a sigh of resignation Moses answered it. The scrambled voice of the night before croaked, "So you boys thought that maybe I'd forgotten you?"

"One can always hope can't one?"

"Yes, yes, keep your hopes up. I wouldn't want you to despair. You're much too important to my project."

"So you've decided to make us pawns in our sick little game as well?"

"Oh you just don't understand. It's not a little game, it's grandiose! Fantastic!"

"Yeah, so when does the fun start?"

"You're a little slow aren't you? It's started already. Now walk on over to the north bound platform of the red line. You'll get off when I tell you. Bye for now."

The three of them left the mission revival cum art deco interior of Union Station and descended into the grey concrete austerity of the subway. They looked around them but didn't see anyone who might be either murderous cult members or undercover, police. Just tourists in shorts and sandals with faces tinted green by eye shade caps, tired and beaten night shift workers, and heavily medicated SSI recipients wasting their time.

They bought tickets and got on the next train. As it rode north the car gradually emptied until they were almost alone. Just before they got to the end of the line Moses' phone rang again. "I hope you enjoyed your ride. Be sure to save your tickets so you can count them as a business expense," chirped the voice with a mocking intonation that the scrambler failed to mask.

"Oh, it was loads of fun. Where to now?"

"Go upstairs fool, it's the end of the line. And don't hang up."

They emerged into the bounty of light and space surrounding the Metro station and blinked their eyes while trying to get their bearings. A pair of Mormons, wearing dress shirts and ties and sheltering themselves from the sun with a silver parasol, had the air of emissaries from another dimension. The rest of the people present were dressed in bargain clothes and idling in the shade as if waiting for something uncertain to happen. Moses decided to consult their tormentor on the telephone. "We're at the place in front of the Metro what's next?"

"Give the phone to Mike."

"To Mike?"

"Just a caprice, I've decided to make him leader."

Moses muttered, "depraved freak," and passed the phone to Mike.

"I heard that," retorted the voice, "another black mark next to your name."

Mike took the phone and held it out in front of him as if it were some kind of homing device. "Go to the red and black trash can," he was told. Mike turned and walked over to the receptacle that with its red body and black hood looked a bit like a Star Wars droid stripped of all its futuristic accoutrements. Murphy and Mcbrade hung back warily.

"Now what."

"Put your hand inside."

Mike hesitated. He thought of the device that had sliced off Madrid Ramada's arm. "I don't think I want to do that."

"Oh, come on. Be a sport."

Cautiously Mike reached inside and was relieved when his hand was neither chopped off nor burned to a crisp. "What am I supposed to get?"

"Turn your hand up and you'll find it on the bottom of the hood."

Mike felt something made of plastic with a wire hanging from it taped to the cover's interior and closing his eyes he pulled it out, hoping and praying it wasn't a detonator. He opened his hand to see a cell phone in a black case with a Bluetooth in his hand. Never in his life had something so innocuous caused him such terror. "What do I do now?"

"Just put the headset on, poor fool."

Mike hooked the device to the right side of his head and noticed that the phone was on. He almost tore it off when the voice came through the ear piece. "Now we can be alone together."

"Not my idea of a date."

"Don't be too hasty. Maybe I'm a woman."

"But your voice sounds like a monster."

"Perhaps my scrambler is more sophisticated than you imagined."

"Fine, mister or madam or whatever combination of the two. What do I do now?"

"Head south on Lankershirm. Bring the other two with you."

Mike waved at them to follow. They went to the broad boulevard lined with chintzy office buildings and biblical palms and turned south. The idlers scrutinized them as they past, as if they might be whatever it was they were looking for. The three kept their eyes averted and their faces stoically blank in order to avoid any contact. Just as they were passing out of the territory of the shuffling idlers they ran into a congregation of street preachers who pressed up against them demanding their repentance. "He suffered and died so you don't have to," they intoned.

"Go on, go on, bloody low Protestant bastards," Mcbrade berated them and, as they pushed their way through, he suddenly yelped. "One of them pricked me with something."

Mcbrade was on the point of having words with them but Moses pulled him away, "We've other problems to solve and with your accent none of them will understand a word you say."

He grudgingly continued while muttering under his breath.

Just then the voice in Mike's ear chimed in, "Maybe you'd like some music to accompany you, just like as if this were a film."

"I'd prefer silence."

"But you're just an assistant director while I'm the producer of this flick so..." And then, just as if he knew precisely what would unhinge Mike the most, he began singing nonsense syllables like: "bing ba doddy blip bang foody bar to baddy far so laddy" accompanied by an ukulele.

After few minutes of trudging along through the stifling heat, intensely concentrated upon them by the concrete sidewalks and glass fronted buildings as if they were built for just that purpose, Mike couldn't take it anymore. "Where are you taking us to? Why are you making that gibberish music?"

"Just trying to be entertaining. Anyway you are near your goal. Do you see a bank?"

"Yes."

"Go to it."

Mike went and stood under a ledge like projection on the buildings face that afforded some shelter from the sunlight. Mcbrade and Murphy came and huddled next to him in the patch of shade. "Now what?"

"You see the transformer box in front of you?"

"Yes."

"Tell Mcbrade to put the money in it."

"He'll need a key."

"You've already got it. In the cellphone case."

Mike turned the case over and noticed that something was wedged inside between it and the cell phone, so tight that it was on the point of splintering the case. Mike grabbed Mcbrade's shoulder and shook him out of the torpor that he had sunk into during their walk.

"He wants you to put the money in the box."

"I can't, something's happening to me, I'm too sick," he murmured before collapsing to the ground.

"He can't do it, he looks like he needs an ambulance."

"No! He has trespassed, he must be the one to pay! Pick him up and carry him over there."

Mike turned to Moses for help in getting the ill man on his feet. "He's got to put the cash in that box." As they started towards the box Mike was struck by a sudden feeling that this was a trap. He noticed a pool of some sort of multi-colored viscous liquid in front of the transformer. It might be vomit or it might some sort of conductor. He tried to pull Mcbrade back but somehow he'd recovered enough strength to shake free of his grasp. Even after Mike yanked Moses' hand away he staggered on.

He had put the key in the transformer box's lock and was on the point of turning it when his whole body contracted and convulsed as if some monstrous invisible hand had taken hold of him and shook him. Mike stepped to the side of the transformer away from the puddle and, praying that the rubber soles of his shoes would provide enough insulation, gave Mcbrade a side kick to free him from the contact that was electrocuting him. But the current had done its work, and the cult's latest victim fell to the ground stone dead.

Mike looked at the crumpled corpse and the contorted expression on its face. "That was supposed to be us," he let out.

The voice cackled evilly through the earpiece, "So you two still there? Well that's alright you'll never catch up to me anyway. You can keep the phone, I might want to get in touch with you again."

Mike let loose a barrage of curses but it was all in vain as the line had already gone dead.

Moses' cell phone rang and he answered, "Can't you stop playing your game for just a second? Oh, um I'm sorry detective Ruh I thought it was somebody else, the maniac responsible for all this. Apparently it was all just a set up. He wanted to kill all three of us but he only got Mcbrade. You better send the coroner. You're at the hospital with her? We'll be there in about a half hour." He put away the phone and spoke to Mike, "We've got to go downtown, Lisa Stave wants to speak to us."

TWENTY SIX

They hiked back to the metro station and got a cab. With the help of his dispatcher the cabbie expertly bypassed traffic snarls and they were at the hospital in half an hour. Getting up to see detective Stave proved a bit more time consuming, as they had to talk their way through the heavy security that had been put in place. Eventually they were let into her room. She looked weak, pale, and somehow smaller than before.

Detective Ruh brought them up to date on her medical condition, "The bullet just missed her spinal cord and her kidney but nicked her pancreas. She's going to live but she'll have to spend a month or so in bed. There's something that she wanted to say to you."

He led them to the bedside and Lisa's eye's fluttered open, "So I heard he tried to kill the two of you as well? We should have anticipated that."

"We're still here and we're not going to back off. We're going after these bastards till we get them."

"Maybe you should just give up. Let it go. Let the police take care of it."

"Give up? I'm not going to let my business be destroyed by these maniacs. I'm going to hunt them down and make them pay."

"Is it really worth it? Do you think that you can actually do anything?"

"I've got to."

"Fine, go ahead. I can't force you to close up your business but I'm strongly advising you to do so. I'm not going to have any more official contact with you but I want to talk to Mike alone."

"What have you got to say to him?"

"That's between him and me. Leave us alone." Moses spun around and walked off, but Ruh hesitated. "I'll be all right," Lisa reassured him, "I've just got something to say to him."

When they were alone Mike spoke up, "So what is it?"

"You really should quit this job."

"Why, what else am I going to do?"

"It doesn't matter what. You just need to get away from this job."

"I don't think I can do that."

"Okay, I've warned you. I've got the feeling that this thing is just going to keep on getting bigger and eventually either crush you or make you...."

"Make me what?"

"Make you what you were meant to be."

"What I was meant to be?"

"Yes, you'll be free from all it is that has been keeping you down."

"What the hell are you talking about? You sound kind of like a cult member yourself."

"You know sometimes California seems like one big cult one that you can't quit even if you want."

"I know the feeling."

"Then you'll understand when I tell you that maybe you want to walk away from this one."

"Actually I don't really have anything to lose and you say that if I beat this group I'll be freed. Freed from what exactly?"

"You know what, everything that is haunting you."

"In that case maybe it's worth it. Get well soon."

Lisa managed a feeble smile. "I can already feel myself healing."

At the door Mike gave her one last look but her eyes were already shut.

In the elevator a cell phone began ringing in Mike's pocket and it took him a second to realize that it wasn't his cell phone but that of the chief stalker. Cautiously Mike answered, "Yes, what do you want now?"

"Just calling to have a little chat. Where are you?"

"At the hospital."

"Go to the bench out in front of the main entry and I'll call you back."

Mike hurried through the busy corridors and exiting the hospital went to the bench to sit down. He felt like an open target. When it rang again, he jabbed at the screen with a trembling finger and the voice came on.

"I told you our game wasn't over, and I meant it."

"What the hell do you want with me?"

"A master uses the pieces available as he can."

"I'm not playing any more with you."

"What about Lisa?"

"What about her?"

"Something worse could always happen to her."

"She's heavily protected."

"By the police?"

"Yes."

"What makes you so sure that some of us aren't with the police?"

Mike's hand shook even harder but now with fury, "If you do something to her I promise I'll track you down."

"Track me down huh? You've been doing a great job of that so far."

"I'll find you somehow."

"You'll never find me, and anyway if you follow my instructions no harm will come to her."

"What do you want from me?"

"Nothing right now, just keep this phone with you at all times and don't tell anyone that you have it." The voice then hung up leaving Mike on the concrete bench to wonder what role it was holding in reserve for him.

KILLEBRITY

When he got home there was a message waiting for him on his voice mail. It was Moses telling him that he should take the next few days off. At first Mike was elated, a vacation from the hell he'd lived through was desperately needed, but after lying on his bed for an hour or so despair took hold of him anew. Somewhere out there a malefic mastermind was plotting new horrors and now it wanted to make him part of them.

He tried going out to a park or a beach but it only made things worse. The mass of carefree revelers seemed to have been called together to taunt his desolation. He pondered Lisa's words. How could defeating this menace save him? Win or lose, the longer he struggled against it the farther he would be led from the simple joys of the people cavorting on the sand and the grass.

The only answer left to him was alcohol so he bought a supply of liquor and passed his time drinking and staring at the walls. After a period of inebriation whose duration was very vague, the phone rang. He looked at it ring. It seemed to be ringing unnaturally loud and hard. So loud that he felt like covering his ears with his hands. So hard that it seemed to make the nightstand it was on shake. He dreaded the news that the call might bring but the ringing was so awful that he was compelled to answer.

He picked up the receiver and Moses came on the line. "So you all rested, refreshed and recovered? There's something that's come up."

"What kind of something? Is someone else dead?"

"No, nothing like that. I'm having a meeting with someone that has a plan to stop the killers."

"What kind of plan?"

"I'll fill you in when we meet with him tomorrow. Do you got something to write this down with?"

Mike pulled a pen and a pad of paper out of the nightstand's drawer, "Yeah, go ahead."

"NTM agency sixty nine sixty nine Beverly Boulevard at ten o'clock."

"What floor?"

"Just ring the button and you'll be told where to go."

"Is this a new client or something?"

"I don't want to talk about it over the phone, you'll find out tomorrow."

Without any further explanation Moses hung up leaving Mike ruminate about whatever the "plan" might be. If this was a new client then Mike couldn't very well meet them with a hangover. His alarm clock read 4pm, so he had eighteen unbearable hours of sobriety to endure before he would find out what kind of new adventure he was going to be thrown into.

He decided to go to the web café across the street to find out who the person or people he was meeting tomorrow might be. He lurched across the street being nearly run over twice and tripped while going through the door landing on his face. Behind the counter was someone who looked like the same girl who had been there the last time he'd come in, except her hair had changed color, her piercings had moved and she was wearing glasses that magnified her eyes.

She directed him to a cubicle and he sat down and did a google search for NTM agency. They had an austere minimalist web site that a designer had been well paid to conceive, but it didn't give out much information about their activities. "The privacy of all our clients is strictly respected," a bold notice on the homepage read. The full names of their agents weren't given either, just their first names, an email, and a secretary's phone number.

So now a mysterious talent agency was going to help them in their fight with a secret cult of celebrity murderers. Things just kept getting stranger and stranger. He looked some more but couldn't find any articles detailing the activities of NTM. The only bit of insight he found was on a forum for aspiring actors. A member wanting to know how to get representation from the low profile group was told, "You don't pick NTM. They pick you."

Had NTM, whoever they might be, decided to pick him for some obscure reason? He really didn't feel like being on the team. After trying to rub the bad ideas out of his head by massaging his temples he went to pay. The cashier smiled at his evident discomfort and Mike threw her a scowl. "So you think the way I feel is funny do you?"

"No I don't. I was just thinking that if you're going to self-medicate you should do it right."

"And what's the right way according to you?"

"How about some herb? It'll set you right."

"No, that stuff makes me paranoid, and believe me I have so much to be paranoid about right now that it'll make my head explode."

"Well we wouldn't want your head to explode would we? But what I've got is hundred percent Indica. It will chill you straight out."

"So, you want to sell me some grass?"

"No, I was just going to suggest that we go out back and smoke some together."

"You'd just leave the store unattended?"

"I've got somebody," she said and then turned her head towards the back and shouted, "hey Johnny, come keep an eye on things."

An old wino limped out of a murky storage area. He smiled and nodded his head wordlessly at Mike and the girl before sitting down on a stool next to the cash register.

The girl led him into the same darkness the old man had emerged from.

"Your name is Mike right? I remember from your ID. My name is Dog Vomit."

"Dog Vomit?"

"Yes, sad to say, my parents were punks."

"Mine were Republicans and Catholics."

"Oh, too bad."

"I've learned to live with it."

They emerged into a small courtyard made of the backs of the surrounding buildings. The ideal place to spring a trap Mike thought. She turned to him and took a pre-rolled joint out of a metal case.

"That old man is the owner's uncle or something, he'll watch over things while we get high."

After several hits Mike felt himself slipping away into a calmer less threatening world. All the dark forces he felt were menacing him faded away into insignificance. Freed from the burden of fear that had been crushing him he looked around him with a new sort of vision. The squalid courtyard seemed imbued with some sort of magic.

"Wow," Mike gasped, "that really hit the spot."

"I knew that it would," Dog Vomit murmured, "I used to drink all the time to get away from all my ugly memories. This stuff saved me from cirrhosis."

Mike found himself staring into the enlarged eyes of Dog Vomit. He pulled her face towards his until they were kissing. He began caressing her slim body. Within seconds they were having sex against a cinder block wall. It felt like what he was meant to do. Everything else, the war, his job, the cult, all seemed trivial. As it ended he stared up into the gray brown clouds above and an acidic rain began pattering his face. He felt for the first time that he belonged in Los Angeles. He was at home there as much as a tiger was in the jungle or a shark was in the sea and no matter what was to come he would survive. The girl then led him back into the store and bid him goodbye as if nothing had happened.

TWENTY SEVEN

Mike floated back home and lay on the bed enjoying a pleasant buzz before passing out and sleeping until the alarm woke him the next morning. He got dressed groggily and hoped that none of the smell of yesterday's smoke had clung to him. He was lucky enough to get a seat by the window on the bus but, as chance would have it, a morbidly obese woman sat down next to him, her blubber pressing against him repulsively.

She began jabbering on the cell phone with some girl friend of hers about all the men in her life. He tried to block the conversation out of his mind but it oozed its way in. Soon his brain was filled with vile images of his fleshy fellow passenger being vigorously penetrated by a pack of chubby chasers. He tried to get up and go to the other end of the bus but he was trapped by her folds of lard and she refused to stand up. He eventually climbed over the seat in front of him and, realizing that he had gone well past his stop, jumped off the bus.

Having had his fill of mass transportation he walked back to the address Moses had given him. 6969 Beverly Boulevard turned out to be a mock Elizabethan apartment building. "I've screwed up again," he groaned, certain that he had gotten the number wrong. He decided he might as well check and see before calling Moses back and admitting his mistake.

As he was trying the handle of the front door an elderly man in a powder blue jump suit with a tiny dog in his hands came out. "Go away," he snapped with a sour expression on his face. "We don't want any."

"I've got an appointment with the NTM agency," stated Mike meekly.

The man smiled broadly displaying what were either remarkably well preserved teeth or very expensive implants. "Oh, why didn't you say so," he said soothingly, holding the door wide open for Mike and leading him inside. "They're in the penthouse suite," he pointed at the topmost black Bakelite button on the copper panel of the speakerphone. "I'm sure you're exactly what they're looking for," he assured Mike before continuing on his way to walk his dog.

Mike rang the button. A confident, businesslike, young female voice answered, "Good morning, NTM agency."

"Yes, this is Mike Johnson. I've got an appointment with you."

"I'll buzz you in, it's the top floor."

Mike stepped into the building's lush interior where gold and white ceiling ornaments sparkled above a wine red carpet and sea green walls. He mounted the more modern but still stately elevator that bore him smoothly and swiftly upwards. Getting off at the highest story, he found himself in a reception room lit by Tiffany lamps and adorned with darkly themed romantic paintings.

A woman who looked like she might well be the one whom he'd spoken with on the speakerphone greeted him. "Take a seat Mister Johnson, they'll be with you shortly." Mike sat down tenderly on one of the antique chairs lining the wall and gazed at the paintings.

Epic events from ancient times were unfolding on their surfaces. They made Mike feel all that much more insignificant. Nobody was ever going to paint any such portraits of the battles he'd been in. Most people were probably going to try and forget that they had even happened.

After he had been sufficiently humbled by the décor something on the secretary's desk buzzed and she called out to him. "You may go in now Mister Johnson," she ordained and pointed to a door with thick red sound proof padding and a light blinking above it. Mike went through this formidable entry dreading what he might meet.

The first person he saw was Moses, who was seated in a plush easy chair and seemed to be in an uncharacteristically good humor. He was in the midst of a conversation with a lanky man in a black suit with slicked back white hair seated behind a massive oak desk. By pointing a bony finger, he indicated that Mike should sit in a chair besides Moses. "This event might just be a smashing success on several levels if done right," the gaunt man intoned, "but the security must be foolproof."

A man standing looking out a corner window whom Mike hadn't noticed chimed in, speaking in a curious accent, "Yes, it must be safe, absolutely safe." He then turned towards the center of the room and Mike recognized the famous lead singer of the hit band from Wales whose name he couldn't quite remember. "We can't have a single person getting hurt, not a one." He then walked over to Mike to introduce himself. "I'm Alun Wynn and you must be Mike Johnson."

"That's me, Mike Johnson, I've heard of you of course."

"Not a fan I wager."

"Well, I've heard your songs."

"Everybody has, in a lift or something."

"An airlift? They never played any music in any air lifts I've been in."

Alun guffawed good naturedly, "I meant to say an elevator, that's what you call them don't you. Anyway, I imagine in your theater of operations they preferred Black Metal or something 'destroy' what."

"There was always some Arabic music playing. It got on our nerves so we listened to something loud to drown it out."

"I see, of course things must have been more complicated than I can imagine."

"Complicated, yes that's how it was. Anyway, why am I here?"

The man behind the desk stood up and walked over to Mike, "I'm mister Finister the director of this agency. After some hesitancy we've decided to include you in this project."

Mike shook hands with Finister and Wynn and hesitated a bit before replying. "I've got two questions; what project and why me? Aren't there any better people for this job?"

Finister fixed his steely regard upon Mike. "We're putting together something that we hope will end these murders."

"Oh? What might that be?"

"An event, a big event."

"The only event that I could imagine stopping these crazies is a mass suicide."

The room fell silent at this declaration and Alun Wynn walked over to the window and after glancing outside turned back to Mike. "For you what is an event?"

"I don't know, something that happens, something important."

"Yes, but why are some of the things that happen important enough to be events and others not?"

"I don't know. It's just like that."

"It's not just like that. Events don't happen they are made. They have the significance and meaning with which their participants endow them."

"Yeah, I guess that's how it works."

"And what truly makes them events is how they change things. How they alter people's way of seeing the world."

"Um, right, so?"

"The lunar landing was nothing more than some men visiting a useless rock, Woodstock just some hippies getting high and fucking in the mud, and Altamont a common biker brawl that ended with someone getting knifed."

"You obviously know the business that you're in better than I do, no wonder you've made so much money from it."

A keen undertone rose in Alun's voice, "So you think I have too much? Much more than I merit?"

"No, no I didn't mean that at all sir. I'm sure you've worked hard for what you have and you deserve every bit of it."

"Actually, deserving has nothing to do with it. It's more a matter of needing. What I do is not nearly as vital as what I am, and to be what I am I must have what I have. I'm not just a man but a symbol, a symbol of hope, justice and freedom among other things. I have to shine with glory, and living a beautiful life, a life of fabulous luxury, is essential to that."

Mike was completely thrown off by the super pop star's spiel. "I have to admit I've never thought of things in quite that way before."

"You see! I can change things. I can bring another world into being, a world where people won't feel the need to kill."

"You think this change will stop these people?"

"I'm going to bring change into this world by doing what I do best, I'm going to perform and I'm going to make everybody part of my performance. When these crazed murderers see this they'll know that they can never win. They probably think now that what they're doing is somehow revolutionary, that we're the piggies and we need to be brought down. But this event I'm going to organize will make everyone realize that we celebrities are a part of them. We're a manifestation of their hopes, dreams and aspirations."

Mike knew that the mega pop star was simply regurgitating some prewritten speech, but it was recited with such intensity and conviction that it moved something within him, something buried deep beneath the layers of cynicism and misanthropy that had built up around his soul like a callus, and he realized with discomfort that he still had a need to believe.

Alun peered ardently into Mike's eyes, as if his gaze could penetrate all the defenses that Mike had erected to protect himself from the pitiless life he had lived. "You know it's possible, you know it can be so."

Mike squinted painfully back at the multi-millionaire musician as if he was looking towards a piercing light. "I don't know anything anymore. After what I've just been through nothing seems to mean anything anymore."

Alun slapped Mike congenially on the back. "You! You're the audience I'm trying to reach, all the lost and alienated. I'm going to make it all mean something to you. Come and look."

He walked over to a table on which some bulky form lay concealed beneath a sheet. He whipped it away to reveal a model of the Hollywood Bowl. Everyone gathered around it as though it was a freshly unwrapped Christmas present. "This is where it will happen," Alun boldly announced, "this is where it will all change."

Moses inspected the lay out. "This place will be hard to secure."

Alun picked up a pointer. "The architect I've commissioned has designed a wall of bullet proof glass that will fit into the proscenium arch." He tapped the tip of the pointer on a clear semi-circular piece of plastic representing an anti-sniper screen. "The arch itself will be reinforced so we'll be protected from the explosion of any bomb, no matter how powerful." He rapped soundly on the roof of the bowl and grinned. "As long as it isn't nuclear of course. But if these bastards have nukes then we're all fucked." He looked up to see if his wit was appreciated and the others forced themselves to smile.

When no one proffered any comments Alun continued with his presentation. He waved the pointer over the seating area, which upon closer examination was seen to contain tens of thousands of tiny figurines representing the audience. "Every spectator will be supplied with a small video camera that will transmit its images to these screens." He ran the tip of the telescoping chrome stick over an array of plastic rectangles surrounding the seating gallery and facing inward. "The crowd will be able to film each other as they experience our show."

Mike felt an opportunity to demonstrate the smidgen of understanding of electronic imagery that he had picked up in an audiovisual studies class. "And the technical director will switch between all the video feeds to choose which shots are worth displaying."

Alun shook his head slowly with his eyes closed. "You really don't understand what we are trying to do here. To have someone choose whose faces will be splashed upon the screens would be imposing something. That's not at all what we want to do. We want this to be a spontaneous expression of the gathering's feelings. Beside there will be too many feeds, it would be humanly impossible to select the dozen or so most absorbing amongst them."

Admonished, Mike delicately expressed his interest. "Well, it's definitely beyond me. How will it be done then?"

Alun waved the pointer in the air triumphantly. "We shall take advantage of the latest technology. You've heard of facial recognition programs, haven't you?"

They all nodded their assent.

"What we shall be using is one of the latest derivations of that. An application that analyzes people's faces not in order to compare them with mug shots that are on file but to identify individuals who are experiencing emotional extremes, such people being more likely to commit crimes, harm

cap, liberating some foam that drenched his fingers. He licked it away and took a swig, all the while keeping his eyes glued to the black box.

He put the beer back down and gingerly picked it up. Just having something from her in his hands helped chase away the demons that were tormenting him. He hesitated to open it. The neatly folded gift paper and delicately tied bow were a tiny testament that someone in this world was thinking of him with gentle thoughts. Though he was curious to discover its contents, he couldn't bear to tear it apart.

After turning it over a few times he discovered a small card stuck on it that he hadn't noticed because it had the same color and texture as the wrapping paper. He unfolded it. "Lite me up," it read. Mike was at a loss. Was he supposed to burn the package without finding out what it contained? He couldn't bring himself to do that.

A slight tug on the ribbon undid it and the paper unfolded almost by itself to reveal a cigarillo box. Mike wonder if it might not be some sort of joke. Perhaps something was set to spring out of it. He placed it back on the table and, after a few more swallows to strengthen his resolve, he lifted the lid. The scent of cannabis rose to his nostrils. Inside the box lay a row of expertly rolled spliffs. For a moment he was disappointed; it seemed like a rather mercenary offering. After wondering for a bit about the spirit that it might have been given in, he realized that it might be meant as a sort of memento of their moment together.

He had to smoke one right away. It would be almost as if they were together again. He remembered the lighters and glass pipes he had uncovered under the sink when trying to fix a leak. A meth smoking former tenant had left them behind when the police had dragged him away. Not wanting to get his fingerprints on any hard drug paraphernalia he had let them lie where they were. He went and got a lighter. Soon the curative smoke was filling his lungs.

A cloud of it gathered above his head. He looked up at it and could almost see Dog Vomit floating on its fluffy white billows like an angel watching over him from heaven. A few stray molecules of THC present in the weed tried poking him with twinges of paranoia but he maintained his calm. He was infused with a feeling that rendered him immune to anxiety.

Though he was shielded from angst he was hit with the munchies. He felt hungrier than if he had come back from a long patrol on Thanksgiving, and turkey and stuffing was waiting for him as a sweet reminder of home. He thought of the meagerly stocked shelves of the shop where Dog worked. Not the healthiest or most appetizing choice of snacks but he was ready to eat anything.

The Los Angeles that lay awaiting him when he stepped outside was more unreal than ever, but he didn't feel in the slightest way threatened. He simply gazed at it in wonder. The old man in the shop nodded knowingly at him when Mike came in the door, and he waved discretely back. Pot heads made much better customers than tweakers, and their inoffensive vice was to be welcomed and encouraged.

Mike examined the racks of canned, bottled and packaged food. Though the packages of potato chips looked enticing, there wasn't any dip to go with them among the condiments, but there were jars of mayonnaise and mustard. The outline of a recipe was forming in his mind. Looking around he noticed a neglected array of vegetables in the corner. Most of them were a bit shriveled but the onions seemed fresh enough. He grabbed some and a can of tuna.

Gathering up all the ingredients he brought them to the counter and then pulled a six pack of Rolling Rock out of the cooler. This time the owner's relative graciously allowed Mike to pay for his purchases and then stacked it all neatly in a paper bag. His stomach already growling in anticipation of the feast, Mike hurried home.

He put the beer in the fridge and laid out the makings of his meal on the counter. Opening the can of tuna, he dumped the fish meat in the bowl and broke it into crumbs with a spoon. Then he crushed the potato chips inside their sack and poured them in. Next he chopped the onions before scraping them off the cutting board into the bowl. Finally he added in some mustard and mayonnaise. He carried the mixture and a beer over to the table and dug in.

He sat down and began eagerly spooning it into his mouth. He digested it with a pure feeling of visceral pleasure. No king seated before a banquet given by his court ever feasted more grandly. No infant in its mother's arms ever fed so serenely. He was driven by a savage ravenousness like that of hyenas devouring some carrion well ripened by the sun of the savannah.

He quickly scarfed down the entire bowl. He kept on sipping beer straight from the bottles. Every swallow drenched his tongue with tasty hops and malt. If he had been asked, he wouldn't have been able to put into words how he was feeling, but he knew he wanted it to go on. The thought that it might be nothing but a fleeting chemically induced state began coursing through his synapses. He feared that there was nothing but a flimsy layer of cannabinoids insulating him from the stark terror that had been haunting him for much too long. However artificial it might be it had to be reinforced.

He lit up again and took a deep toke holding the slowly burning joint reverently in his fingers, as if it were some sacred stick of incense whose fumes could ward off the forces of darkness. The substances his bronchi were absorbing were not quite capable of reviving the euphoria that Mike had felt but it induced an appeased contentment. The simple snack had satiated him, and he lay down his head as blood rushed to his stomach to digest it.

TWENTY NINE

In what could have been seconds or centuries later he was awakened by a furious pounding on the door. In his confused state of mind he was convinced that it must be the police, coming back to check whether the crank abusing former tenant had taken up residence there again. He gulped down the two roaches and squirreled the lighter and the box of spliffs away in his jacket.

He crept to the peephole and saw Moses' enlarged distorted face glaring at him. He hastily opened the door and let his employer in.

"What the hell happened to you?"

"Nothing, I was just taking a nap."

"A nap? It's ten motherfucking AM in the morning!"

"But I had a day off."

"Yes, one day. I don't want to know how you spent it but it's time to get to work. You've already missed the orientation this morning."

"What day are we?" Mike said groggily.

"Damn! What have you done to your mind? It's Friday, the day of the concert. Everybody's there. Everybody's getting it ready. Everybody but you."

As if he were peering through a thick bank of fog, Mike could make out nothing but a vague outline of Moses' face. It was as though the last forty eight hours had been a decade of exile in some foreign land and now he had been spirited back to his native country, all its customs having become nonsense to him. Moses' anger was the most meaningless of all. But then, like the almost forgotten memory of a childhood scolding so severe that it seared forever the image of authority upon the spirit, the reality of it came back. Moses was his boss and he was there to give him orders, and no matter what perils those orders might lead him through, he was condemned to follow them.

The work that had been accomplished at the Hollywood Bowl in only two days was impressive. A gleaming wall of bullet proof glass shielded the stage like a force field. The imposing array of giant television screens rose above the auditorium. Thousands of stage hands milled about adjusting equipment and adding finishing touches to the décor. Mike stared at it all feeling lost.

Moses grabbed him by the shoulder and shook him. "You've got to snap out of it! You're supposed to be my assistant." He handed Mike a small walky-talky. "People are going to be calling you and you'll have to deal with their calls. Even though you don't have any idea what's going on here you've got to act like you're in charge. I've got other things to take care of. When there's a message for the assistant chief of security you answer and tell them that whatever they're asking about is okay." He then pulled a folder out of his briefcase. "Here are some diagrams and layouts of this place. In case you need to know where something is."

Befuddled, Mike looked at the folder and the walky-talky and nodded.

Without another word Moses stormed off leaving Mike to handle whatever problems might arise.

Mike listened to the traffic on the radio to get an idea of what was going on, but as he didn't have any idea of who anyone was or what they were supposed to be doing, it was all like trying to decipher some enemy's code. Some work crew or other needed to go someplace and do something and some other people had to be ready for it. Suddenly a call came for him, "chief of fire safety for assistant chief of security, over."

Cautiously, Mike pushed the button to answer, "assistant chief of security, over."

"Are all the fire extinguishers in place?"

Mike was completely flustered. If he answered no then the chief of fire safety would check the extinguishers, and when he found that they were in place and functioning he'd know that Mike had no clue to what he was doing. Anyway, Moses had said to say that everything was okay. So with as confident a voice as possible Mike answered, "All extinguishers checked."

"You sure?"

"Of course."

"Who checked them?"

It was as though a trap had been purposely laid for Mike. He didn't know who this chief of fire security was but he hated him. He was probably someone who couldn't make it as a real fire fighter. If he were truly diligent he'd go and check the goddamn extinguishers himself. Now he had put Mike in a difficult place. Mike came to a quick decision. "What fire extinguishers?"

"The ones backstage of course."

Mike saw a way out. "I checked them myself."

"You did? Were the seals indicating that they had been properly filled intact?"

This bastard seemed to take himself for Mike's boss or something. He decided to put him back in his place. "I know what a full fire extinguisher is supposed to look like dammit. Now you do your job and let me do mine."

"You don't have to take it like that. I'm just following procedure."

Mike imagined that "Following Procedure" was probably the fire safety chief's nickname. "Okay, noted, copy," Mike stated concisely in order to rid himself of the pest, then he made his way back stage to make sure that the extinguishers were as they should be. He found them with one of the diagrams Moses had left him, and when he got back out to his post at the right of the stage the show had already begun.

To reverberating guitar riffs an elaborate laser light display lit up the sky. On the video screens the rainbow hued faces of audience members were gazing upward with childlike wonder. For Mike it was like being a eunuch forced to watch porn. He felt nothing in common with the senselessly undulating mass of humanity. It all seemed vaguely threatening. He needed to smoke another joint.

Finding a hidden niche he lit up. After a few tokes the spectacle seemed kitsch and amusing. It was kind of like watching a lava lamp. The cast of celebrities sung a series of ballades promising things they could never deliver, like hope, joy, liberty and redemption. Fortunately, the two hour long program passed quickly, and they were at the ovation when the fire security chief called Mike back.

"Fire security chief for assistant chief of security, over."

Mike thought about ignoring the man but then reluctantly answered. "Assistant chief of security, over."

"Are the shell doors clear? The cast will be leaving the shell in a few minutes, and we need them to be clear."

Mike decided not to let himself be trapped this time. "Is that my job? To know if the shell doors are clear?"

"Well, if you had been at the orientation you'd know what your job is."

Mike exploded, "You're not my goddamn boss! I don't fucking work for you!"

The self-important fire security chief became suddenly conciliatory, "I'm just trying to make sure that everything's going okay. I'd check the exits myself but I'm stuck in the crowd. The fireworks are supposed to go off in a few minutes, and the shell doors need to be clear in case something goes wrong."

Resignedly Mike replied, "So what do you want me to do?"

"Could you go back and check them out please?"

"Sure, can do, copy."

With the diagram he had used before Mike found his way to a shell door. He wondered how he was supposed to know if it was clear. Not wanting to venture into another conversation with the fire security chief, he rattled its nob and found it was locked. He pushed against it but it was if were frozen solid. He began to get the feeling that something was very wrong. He ran from door to door and found them all sealed tight.

He had no choice but to call for help. "Assistant chief of security for fire security chief, over."

"Fire security chief over."

"All the shell doors are blocked."

"How the hell did that happen?"

"I don't know." Mike examined the door he was in front of and saw what looked like melted metal along its edge. "It appears to have been welded shut."

"Welded shut? How the hell could that happen?"

Mike felt the weldment and it was still warm. "Seems like somebody just did it."

"Damn, how are the cast going to evacuate?"

"I've no idea."

"Let me think, um, there are ladders."

"A ladder?"

"Yes, there are ladders from the stage to the halo."

"The halo?"

"Yes, that's the walkway inside the shell. There are other ladders on the outside of the shell that lead up to the halo. Go and find them and call me back."

Mike remembered passing a ladder leading upward and hurried back to it. "I'm at the ladder."

"Climb up to the halo."

Mike threw the folder aside and, sticking the walky-talky in his pocket, rapidly mounted the ladder that led up the side of the shell. He then passed through an opening to gain access to the walkway where he looked down upon the performers. They were bowing graciously as the audience applauded wildly.

"I'm on the halo."

"Okay, go to the ladders that slide down to the stage."

After searching a bit Mike found an extensible ladder hanging from the walkway but to his horror discovered that the rungs had been attached to each other by a long padlock. "The ladder's been locked."

"Locked? Who the fuck would do that?"

"I've no idea." But Mike had a good idea. This clearly had the mark of one of the cult's murderous plots.

"There should be a tool box up there, get it and try to break the lock."

After fumbling around in the shadows Mike stumbled over the toolbox and lugged it over to the blocked ladder. He had been pounding on it with a hammer to no avail for about a minute before the fire security chief called him back. "Have you broken the lock?"

"No, it's too sturdy."

"Try sawing it."

Mike got out a hacksaw and was about to cut into the lock's shackle when the fireworks went off. He watched the trail of their fuses rising into the sky and was perplexed when instead of exploding into balls of colorful light they fell back towards the ground. Then a terrible realization struck him. The shells were falling towards the audience. Twenty feet over the heads of the back row they burst with a white hot glow that Mike knew well; willy peter, white phosphorus.

Flaming spectators came running down the aisles while others thrashed about as the chemical fire consumed them. Thousands of burning faces screamed their last on the giant screens surrounding the bowl. As another salvo of deadly shells took to the air a panicked mass swarmed towards the stage. The cast of performers, who had so recently been bowing in triumph, huddled together in fear upon finding the shell doors blocked.

KILLEBRITY

As the barrage of deadly missiles advanced a human wave piled up against the bullet proof screen. Soon it collapsed inwards and the audience found themselves standing upon the very personalities they had waited for hours in line to see. From the vantage point of the halo walkway Mike looked on in horror and helplessness as they died, squirming beneath the glass like amoebae under a laboratory slide.

THIRTY

Three hours later Mike found himself in a concrete walled interview room handcuffed to a metal table. Across from him, his face a callous mask, sat detective Ruh. He looked down at some photos on the table and, after spreading them out so that the surface was transformed into a mass of pain and suffering, he turned his daunting gaze up towards Mike.

"So, why don't you tell me how you're involved in all this?"

"I just happened to be working there."

"I hear things like that all the time; 'I just happened to be passing by', 'I was visiting a friend in the neighborhood', or even something completely stupid and unbelievable like 'I got lost and was trying to find my way', but when they happen to be in the wrong place at the right time as much as you have it's no longer possible to put it down to happenstance."

Mike looked back at Ruh through bleary eyes. "It's all like some sort of voodoo or something; like I'm the victim of a spell or a curse."

"Hum, that's a new one. Maybe you can plead not guilty by reason of black magic."

Mike hung his head in dismay. "I already feel condemned. The trial will be nothing but a formality."

Ruh gathered the photos together and stood up, "Well then, I'll just turn you over to the people in the formalities department." With a final contempt filled look at Mike he quit the interview room, slamming the door and turning the lock with a terminal twist.

Alone, cuffed to the table, Mike pondered upon the chain of events that had led him to where he was. What struck him most was the fatalism of it all. It was as though he'd been doomed from the beginning to finish. How could he have known? Nothing remotely like what had happened to him had ever happened to anyone. He replayed the events in his head as if it were all a chess match, and changing a move could have resulted in a less total defeat. But it always ended with him where he was, alone, accused of terrible crimes, and with no one to come to his defense.

He had been playing this game over and over in his mind when the door opened again. It was Moses and detective Ruh. Ruh undid his handcuffs and led him to processing. When he was released he followed Moses to his car. Mike wanted to know what had changed things so dramatically but couldn't get up the nerve to ask. Finally, Moses decided to relieve Mike's consuming curiosity.

"It was Alun."

"Alun?"

"Yes, it was Alun Wynn. He was the mastermind behind the massacre at the Hollywood Bowl."

"But I saw him die with the others."

"That's right, it was a murder suicide."

"But why? Was he insane?"

"Apparently he was simply sick of it all. He thought being a rock superstar was a pathetic charade, and he decided to end it in a big way."

"Was he the leader of the killer cult?"

"No, though he might have had some connection with them. The architect who designed the set with the television screens and the bullet proof glass shield, as well as those responsible for the fireworks that turned out to have been incendiary shells, were working under false identities."

"Were they part of the cult?"

"Who knows? Perhaps Alun simply recruited them and offered them a lot of money; he was certainly rich enough."

"So we know nothing more than we did about them?"

"Nope, but I've got a plan."

"What kind of plan?"

"We're going to infiltrate them."

Mike felt a rumbling in his gut. "And who's going to be fool enough to get mixed up with these psychos?"

Moses turned and looked somberly into Mike's eyes. Mike felt like serpents were writhing in his intestines. "Oh, no not me! I've had my share."

"I believe that they're interested in you and they've been targeting you from the beginning."

"So I quit! I'll find some other job."

"Doing what? Flipping burgers?"

"If that's all I can get."

"You have to understand, you can't quit. These people have you on their list and they're going to follow you wherever you go."

"So what can I do about that?"

"We have to unmask their leader and the best way to do that is to get someone inside their organization."

"What do the police think about this?"

"Fuck the police, I know everything they know. I'm going to put this operation together on my own. Sign on with me, you'll put an end to these motherfuckers and become a hero."

With a sigh of acquiescence Mike laid his skull back against the leather headrest. "I don't feel like being a hero. What do I have to sign?"

"Sign? Shit, I meant that figuratively. There isn't going to be any paperwork for this. Nobody's going to know about this but you, me, and two guys who I've worked with a long time and know I can trust."

"Alright, where do we start?"

"By making contact."

"Where?"

"Don't you know where people make contact nowadays? On the internet."

"Okay, I'll go to the internet café tomorrow."

"Tomorrow? We're going to get to work on this right now."

"But it's three in the morning!"

"So? Do you think people like this keep regular hours? They're too insane to even know night from day. We're going to my loft to get right on this."

Moses paused at the door of his loft to show Mike the combination on a large keypad comprised of all the letters of the alphabet and the numbers 0 to 10. "I'm going to give you the keys to my kingdom. Type in 'LA 90013'."

Mike entered the code and the heavily reinforced door swung inward. Moses then led Mike to the gun safe. "Press your thumb against the scanner." Mike complied and the lock beeped. Moses then typed in a code. "You can open it now." The device recognized Mike's print when he touched the sensor a second time and the bolt slid back unlocking the safe. Moses took a pistol in a holster from his belt. "This is the .32 that I gave you and Ruh confiscated. I'm going to give it back to you now with a slight change."

He swung the cylinder open and ejected the cartridges onto a shelf next to the cabinet. He then held one up for Mike to see. "This is the blank I put in the first chamber." He opened a box of cartridges in the cabinet. "I'm going to put him back away with his inert brothers." Moses set the blank in the box and then opened another box next to it. "And give you six live rounds to play with." Moses reloaded the gun and putting it in the holster handed it back to Mike.

"But it's still only a thirty two."

"Why obsess about caliber? The important thing is to hit your target. Most people get a bullet in them, they stop thinking about shooting you and begin worrying about the blood they're losing."

"But these people are fanatics."

"Precisely why I'm going to send you out with this gun. It will very probably be taken from you, and I don't want to put anything more powerful than that in the hands of murderous maniacs. It will do for defending yourself, but nobody's going to be taking out a hard target with it. If the need arises and I'm not around, you can equip yourself with something more powerful. But for the time being you're going to have to be satisfied with that thirty two."

Mike stuck it back in the holster on his belt. "Well, at least it's light."

"You won't need it right now. You're going to get on the internet and try to attract some attention to yourself."

Moses went to make some coffee and Mike sat down at the desk. The revolver pushed itself uncomfortably into his back so he took it out and laid it next to the computer keyboard. Seeing it lying there, filled with death, gave him the confidence he needed to face whatever was lying in wait for him on the World Wide Web.

He started with a simple search, "celebrity", "killer", and "cult". The addresses of several forums came up. He found one that seemed specifically dedicated towards hatred of the rich and famous; "Killebrity" announced the header in gory red letters. Perusing its threads was sad and dreary work. He got the impression that the majority of the participants were pudgy middle aged virgins living in their mother's basements. They were pathetic and impotent, but the ardor of their fury raged forth from the screen. The deeds of the celebrity killer cult paled in comparison to the horrors that these frustrated freaks longed to inflict upon the objects of their hatred.

The most disturbing thing about the malefic tirades he scanned was that they solicited a certain measure of empathy within him. He too felt alone and powerless in a world that scorned him. He simply lacked their conviction that there was someone out there responsible for his misery. The things that had happened in his life and had led him to where he now was seemed as impersonal as chemical or nuclear reactions and blaming anyone as pointless as accusing electrons, protons or neutrons. He realized that being in combat had given him something that raised him above these grubby masses hammering out their hatred upon their sticky keyboards. It had given him a certain sort of nihilism, a nihilism that might deliver him, a nihilism that might serve him as religious faith and political ideology served others.

Moses came over to him with a bottle of Johnny Walker Black Label. "At a loss for words? Maybe this will help stimulate the loquacious juices." He poured a generous dose of whiskey in Mike's coffee and after downing it Mike raised his hands above the keyboard like a pianist preparing to attack the first chord of a concerto. And as he watched, a flood of bile and bitterness was released. He couldn't believe it was himself typing out the deluge of odium that appeared upon the screen. It was as though some wrathful spirit was howling its hatred through him by automatic writing.

Just after entering his devastatingly acrimonious post of several thousand words Mike realized he'd used his own name. Moses was at the other end of the loft, listening to some music on a pair of earphones while doing some research of his own on a portable computer. Mike waved at him until he caught his attention, and he came to look over Mike's shoulder at the screen.

Moses whistled distressingly. "You sure do have some harsh feelings locked up inside you."

"I just got into character."

"You get into a character that would send a message like that you might not get back out again. But it definitely fits the bill as far as being convincingly filled with crazed hatred."

"The only thing is." Mike pointed at the screen. "I used my own name."

"That's good! These people are sure to already know who you are. You can't hide that. You just have to persuade them that you're dissatisfied enough to defect and join forces with them."

After giving Mike another half cup of whiskey Moses went back to his music and portable, leaving his assistant to deal with all the insanity that his post might stir up. Surprisingly, there was no more activity on the thread that had previously had several entries per minute. Mike's post had somehow hushed the haters. However, his personal page on the forum was humming with activity. It filled with friend requests from the desperately deranged and personal messages proposing unspeakable acts.

After a few hours had passed, activity on the thread picked up again. The first post from a member called "Star Death" read, "He is coming".

Then "Rape the Rich" added, "I'm afraid".

"Have no fear," "Starsky and Bitch" replied. "He is our salvation."

"He is coming for you Mike," "Star Death" continued. "I hope you are still there."

The room suddenly seemed to become darker and colder and Mike shivered as he stared at the screen waiting for a message from the guru of the gruesome sect. After several painfully long minutes a post appeared on the screen from someone with the user name "Fatal Fame." "Welcome Mike, at last you've come to us. You're just the sort of person we've need of. If you could send your resume to the following address..... Ha, Ha, of course we know everything about you already. Perhaps even more than you know about yourself."

At a loss for a suitable answer Mike looked around for Moses and found him hovering over his shoulder. "What should I write?"

"Act like you're a bit lost; ask him why he needs you."

"Why do you need me?" Mike entered.

"We are at war and we need warriors."

"I was never much of a fighter."

"Oh Mike, you've undiscovered resources within you. You've simply to come to us and your true potential will be realized."

"How do I know that you won't simply kill me? You almost killed me twice already if you don't happen to remember; Karl at the Psychotropology Center and with McBrade at the transformer box."

"Think of those as mere tests to see if you met our criteria. And you've passed, splendidly. We want to give you a place of honor within our movement, but first you must tell why you want to be with us."

Mike was again in need of Moses' input. "How should I answer that?"

Moses looked into the reflection of Mike's eyes on the computer screen. "So, how do you feel?"

Mike tried to dodge the question. "Me, I don't really feel much of anything."

Moses placed his hands on Mike's shoulders and kneaded them like a masseur trying to massage away the pain of a knotted muscle. "You've got to tell the truth to these people, or at least as close to the truth as possible. So, tell me how you feel."

Mike stared down at the array of letters on the keyboard with sad eyes; perhaps there was some word hidden there, a magic word that could free him from the terrible spell that held him prisoner. "I feel hopeless, powerless and very much alone."

Moses gave him a congratulatory little pat on the back. "So then write: 'I feel hopeless, powerless and very much alone and I want you to save me from these feelings."

Mike pecked in Moses' words, feeling as though he was stripping naked before a callous doctor for a medical exam. The reply came almost instantly; Mike wondered if it had been prepared in advance and copied and pasted. "You will find hope and power with us and you will never surf the internet alone again. Be at the North West corner of the Cinerama Theater's parking garage at seven o'clock tomorrow evening. We will call you on the phone you kept with further instructions."

Looking a bit confused, Moses reread the post. "The phone you kept? What phone is that?"

Mike lowered his eyes. "The phone that I took from the trash can in North Hollywood."

"You kept it?"

"Yeah."

"But how does he know that you kept it?"

"He called me."

Moses exploded with anger. "He called you? And you didn't say anything about it to me? What the hell is wrong with you?"

"He said that he'd kill Detective Stave if I didn't keep quiet about it."

Moses turned away and paced back and forth several seconds deep in thought. He then turned abruptly back to Mike. "That detective Ruh."

"Ruh?"

"Yeah, there's something about him."

"You think he could be with them?"

"Hell, it seems like anyone could. And what's more he's got it in for me."

"Why's that?"

"We used to be partners."

"Partners? He acts like he doesn't know you're there."

"Our association ended badly. That's why he sometimes doesn't accompany detective Stave. He can't stand to be anywhere near me. It was back when I was working homicide. Ruh and I went to question some punk kid about the murder of one of his cronies, a hardened ex-con."

"If he was a punk why did he have someone like that in his crew?"

"I didn't mean punk like small time. I meant he was a punk rocker, mohawk, safety pins, leather Perfecto jacket, tartan trousers, the whole get up."

"But nobody with any game wants to work with someone dressed up like that, they'd attract too much attention."

"I wondered about that myself until I found out the truth about him. Anyway, all the coffee I was drinking suddenly hit my intestines and I went to the toilet. When I got out the punk is lying on the carpet bleeding and Ruh has a kilo of cocaine in his hand. A couple of minutes later his lawyer knocked on the door; he'd called him when he found out we were paying him a visit. It turns out that the father is some big movie mogul with all kinds of connections. Eventually it was decided to make it all go away. Ruh wouldn't be charged with assault and the punk wouldn't get hit with drug possession. But it hurt Ruh's career bad and he still resents me.

"So what are we going to do?"

"Forget about Ruh for now; we're going to go ahead with this plan. If you can get inside this organization we might get some answers. We've got to stop them soon. The Academy Awards is in only a few days, and with all the shit that's been happening I forgot to tell you that we're the ones pulling security for it."

"Us? Even after all that's happened?"

"We have a contract with them for five years. We've even had special outfits with our logo on them made up." Moses pointed to a rack of charcoal grey suits. "They couldn't get rid of us if they wanted, but if something happens there, I'm finished."

"Maybe we should look around some more on internet to see if there's anything about it. The people connected with this group might let something slip, he takes on some pretty crazy ones that probably aren't so reliable. They could even get drunk and brag about something that hasn't even happened yet."

So Mike and Moses did a google search using words like, mayhem, murder, slaughter, kill, destroy and exterminate coupled with "Academy Awards" and the names of various stars who would be at the presentation. After several hours they came up with nothing solid but they did happen across a rather disturbing video titled "Celebrity Grave Robbers Attack".

It was an excerpt from a webcast dedicated to the odd and unusual. An elderly man in gardening clothes appeared on the screen. A subtitle identified him as the caretaker of "Hollywood Ever After Cemetery". He leaned on a mausoleum and gazed off into the sky as if he might be addressing the souls of the departed that had been entrusted to his care. "It breaks my heart, after all I've done to cherish their memories some sickos come along and dig them up."

"Don't you have watchmen to make sure that this kind of thing doesn't happen?" queried an off camera web journalist.

"Of course we do, but these bastards, whoever they are, seem highly organized. They must be professional criminals."

"Why would professional criminals want the bodies of dead stars?"

"I don't know. Perhaps they're going to sell their body parts on Ebay."

"Ebay? We'll have to watch and see if anything turns up."

The aged caretaker shook his finger at the camera. "It's a disgrace. And the worst of it is that it's not only us. I've spoken with other graveyards around Los Angeles. The same thing has happened to them, dozens of bodies! And the authorities don't seem to care enough to do anything about it."

Moses turned off the computer. "This is becoming too much to process."

Mike sat with his eyes fixed upon the blank screen. "These people are talking about bringing about another world. Pretty strange way to go about it."

"Yeah, and what sort of world would that be?"

"Not a world I would want to live in."

"So you got to be ready to do whatever it takes to stop them. Are you ready?"

"I don't know, but it doesn't seem like I've got much choice."

THIRTY ONE

The following evening at seven o'clock Mike was at the Northwest corner of the second story of the Cinerama Theater parking lot. He was dressed in dark, loose fitting military clothes. Not only would they be useful if he had to move around a lot or hide in the shadows, but they also fit in with the character he was preparing to play, an embittered veteran ready to go on the war path with an extremist group.

As he stood thinking about it he realized that he actually was pretty embittered. He wondered why the idea of joining up with some crazed terrorists didn't really appeal to him. After a few minutes of pondering he came to the conclusion that he was simply too alienated to join in anything, no matter how extreme and anti-social it might be. This train of thought was interrupted by the cell phone ringing. Mike put the Bluetooth in his ear and answered.

"Mike Johnson here."

The scrambled voice came on, "Hello my friend it's so good you've decided to join our little party."

"I'm not really interested in your group so much. I just feel the need to do something, to strike back in some way."

"And you shall have your day of vengeance. There is only so much that a man can do on his own but working with us you can shake this world to its foundations."

"Sounds impressive. What do I do next?"

"There's a black van about ten feet to your left."

Mike spotted the van and walked over to it. "I've found it."

"Good, now feel around the left front wheel well for a magnetic key case."

After fumbling about a bit in the grime Mike felt the case and plucked it out. "I've got it."

"Fine, now get in the car."

Mike did as he was told. He was about to adjust the seat when he noticed that his hand was covered with dirt and grease.

"There's some hand wipes on the dash. Clean yourself up," the voice instructed intuitively.

Mike wondered whether the person on the other end of the line had simply surmised that his hands would need washing after searching for the keys, or if there were miniature cameras installed inside the passenger compartment observing his every move. Regardless, he quickly scrubbed his hands and threw the wipe out the window.

"You know that's littering. We might be killers but we care about the environment," the voice scolded. When Mike began to open the door to retrieve the soiled tissue the voice joshed him, "There's no need to be so blindly obedient, you'll come to see that I've a quite developed sense of humor."

"So how do I know when you're joking?"

"Perhaps I should add a little laugh at the end of every order that I don't wish to be taken at its letter, but I find this world so amusing that I'm laughing all the time."

Mike stifled the feelings he really felt like expressing. "Well, I guess we're going to have a lot of fun together."

"Yes we will. Now start the car and drive towards the Los Angeles convention center. When you get there go to the parking lot."

Mike pulled out, closely followed by Moses who had been waiting in his car a couple of spaces away. As Mike rolled south a sense of impending doom grew within him. What could the cult have in mind for him? Would he be able to convince them that he had come over to their side? What would they do to him if they figured out that he hadn't?

Soon Mike was on the Santa Monica freeway where exceptionally fluid traffic bore him towards his fate. A large banner hanging from the roof of the convention center displayed two giant cartoon characters; one a smiling brown bear, the other a wary looking Asian girl in a sailor outfit. Massed about the entrance were hundreds of people in costumes matching the illustrations on the insignia. The bears and the girls mingled together in front of an illuminated sign announcing, "Pedo Bear meeting Sailor Fuku".

Mike drove past them and to the parking garage. No sooner had he parked than the cult leader called back. "Go to the back of the van," he ordered. Mike did as he was told. "You see the costume?" A bear suit similar to those worn by the conventioneers was hanging from the roof.

"Yes I see it," Mike muttered, looking aghast at the freakish get up, as though it might be the uniform of a condemned man, and he the condemned.

"Get naked and put it on. Keep the Bluetooth on so I can give you directions."

Mike stripped and slipped on the role play outfit. He was at a loss as to what to do with his gun until he found an inside leather lined pocket that seemed designed to serve as a holster. He wondered if all the Pedo Bear costumes were outfitted with such a pocket. It was doubly perturbing to think that not only were grown men walking around dressed as cartoon characters for sexual kicks but that the same men were carrying concealed firearms. He pushed this idea resolutely out of his head and zipped the bear suit closed. It fit snuggly yet comfortably, like a second skin. Just when he began feel a bit sweaty an electric motor switched on with a hum and the inside surface grew cool. Apparently the costume came with built in air conditioning.

As he was trying to imagine the ingenuity that would dedicate such care to something so perverse, the voice came back on the head set. "You have a ticket in the right hip pocket. Use it to go inside."

Walking in the bear suit was a bit difficult, it was as if he had been transformed into a fat animal that normally didn't go about on two feet. But he did have a remarkably large field of view in spite of the encumbering head. As he squeezed past the attendees he was able to get a closer look at them. Layers of make-up had been applied to hide the fact that the oriental adolescents were actually, for the most part, occidental women in their late twenties or early thirties. The Pedo Bears all wore suits identical to his own. As to who might inside them: bored middle aged cubicle slaves, convicted sex criminals, or undercover vice police, he hadn't a clue.

Mike surmised that the goal of making him go through this odd experience was to throw off any followers and, he resigned himself to the fact that Moses had probably already lost his trail. Whatever was lying in wait for him, he'd have to deal with it alone. Using this event to isolate Mike definitely displayed the twisted sense of humor of the evil genius behind the deadly cult. As Mike took in the crowd of adults dressed up for a cartoon carnival, he felt a sneering presence.

Eventually, Mike made his way past the costumed revelers to the entrance and, after presenting his ticket, he stuffed himself through the turnstile and waddled out onto the convention floor. Numerous stands were set up where costumes and accessories complementing the off-beat life style of the convention goers were on sale. Apparently there were some Pedo Bear Sailor Fuku couples present, so there were booths for pastors to unite them and councilors to advise them.

Elsewhere, teams of Bears and Sailors played contact games with no apparent rules that seemed to involve a lot of rolling about, tying each other up, and administering playful punishments. Pushed along by the tide of conventioneers he found himself before a wrestling ring where a Pedo Bear was pitted against several Sailor Fukus. After they had taken him down and carried him away the voice came over the Bluetooth. "Get in the ring."

"What?"

"Do as you're told."

Reluctantly Mike advanced and clambered through the ropes. He found himself facing a deadly serious team of thirtyish wapanese women. They came at him and he back pedaled away almost falling over. Two opponents caught hold of his wrists and bent him over. Another leaped on his back and, getting his neck between her legs, began strangling him with her thighs. The bulky suit made it impossible for him to fight back. After rolling him to the ground, the one behind him squeezed even harder and within seconds he was unconscious.

THIRTY TWO

Mike woke up in a deserted warehouse his head still pounding from lack of oxygen. He hoped his brain hadn't been permanently damaged. When he tried to move he discovered he was strapped down on a sort of operating table. He could only turn his head enough to notice that trays of instruments were laid out on tables to each side of him. Instruments that could be used for surgery, or for torture he grimly acknowledged.

Apart from these dreadful portents he could see nothing but the skeletal metal trusses of an ancient roof and motes of dust suspended in the stark blue-green glow of mercury lamps, which hummed with the sinister tone of a tragic opera's opening note. After several minutes he began to detect some furtive movement at the edges of his vision. Someone or something was skulking about, probably observing him. He realized that whatever it was, it knew that he knew it was there. He, she, or it was merely playing with him to torment him and heighten his terror.

But knowing that it was some sadistic game made Mike no less frightened. The being which had from the beginning used secrecy as one of his primary weapons was continuing to furtively toy with his frayed nerves. Then suddenly he could detect no movement at all, but he could hear a sort of feline padding of feet circling the table. He surmised that his tormentor was turning around him doubled over and on the tips of his toes. They must have received some special training in order to be able to move about so deftly and so low to the ground.

Mike was wondering why this person was exhausting such skills upon someone as insignificant as himself when a head in a skull mask wearing a hood popped up just over face and shouted, "Boo!" Mike's entire body convulsed in a spasm of terror that made the table rattle, and the Halloween costumed head laughed loudly through the voice distorter that Mike had come to know and fear. "Scared you, didn't I? Ha, ha, ha, I see you don't share my sense of humor."

Mike could no longer contain the fury churning inside him. "You mean the humor of a depraved eight year old? The humor of a twisted freak who needs to massacre innocent people?"

His captor laughed again, more softly than before, and Mike realized his mistake. The man behind the spectral disguise had been playing with him in order to provoke such an outburst, and now he knew he had never had any intention of defecting to his ranks. "So, is that how you really feel about me? Too bad, I was hoping we might be friends. But never mind, we can still work together. I've found that some of my best collaborators are people who deep inside hate and despise me but are forced to serve me against their wishes. I'm foreseeing that ours will be the most fruitful collaboration I've yet had. And, as we'll be joining forces, you must know my name. I'm known as Jolly Roger, but you can just call me Jolly." Jolly then reached across and squeezed Mike's index finger with a rubber gloved hand.

"You can torture me, or you can kill me but I'll never work for you. 'Jolly Roger'? Why don't you move to Ethiopia and try being a real pirate?"

"We've found our happy hunting grounds right here. Are you sure you don't want to join our little party? 'Party' for us here and now includes two definitions of the word; a joyful gathering and a political movement. Because though you might not have grasped it yet our little group is very political in a certain sense. A sense that, though it might now be obscured by the randomness of our actions, shall manifest itself over time."

"Oh, so you've read some long books that you didn't understand and now you feel your depraved needs to wreak mayhem have some deep meaning. You're truly a pathetic freak. I think there are probably several million just like you trolling the web from their mother's basement."

"Sorry but you're so wrong for several reasons; primero, this is California and people don't have basements, secundo, if you'd ever met my mother you'd know that living with her, even if I was heavily medicated, is not a possibility, and tertio, I'm out here in the world doing my freaky thing and bringing it all back home where it belongs, and those millions in the basements lust after nothing so much (not even Oriental web porn) as marching in my army."

"That's real scary, a host of pudgy neckbeards going to war."

"Yes, it's true, the quality of my recruits often leaves something to be desired, but I've got my pick from amongst all those millions and some of them have got enough potential to be molded into the sort of soldiers I need. Besides that I've many ways of getting people to do what I want, as you're about to discover."

Upon that ominous note he slipped out of Mike's view and an electric motor hummed. The table he was attached to began slowly pivoting upward, raising his head so he could look out upon the desolate interior of the vast ruined hangar like structure. When he had reached vertical the bed stopped with a click and he saw something rolling towards him from the depths of the shadows.

As it got nearer Mike could make out a figure on a surgical table like his own, slanted at forty five degrees as it might be in an operating theater for the benefit of students come to watch a procedure. It was being pushed along by two of Jolly Roger's acolytes clad as he was except that one wore a deep purple cloak and the other a crimson. Mike speculated that this might be indicative of their rank within the odious organization and shivered at the thought of the horrors one must commit to rise in its monstrous hierarchy. For simplicity's sake, he mentally catalogued them as Red Igor and Purple Igor.

As they approached he remarked that the person on the table was a slim female and as they came into the light a grisly realization hit him; it was Dog Vomit. Her panicked struggles against the restraints made the table rattle like a cage with something frantic in it and her eyes, wide with terror, locked pleadingly upon Mike's gaze as the gag in her mouth made muffled grunts of her screams. Jolly's twin Igors positioned her about ten feet in front of Mike and then the one in crimson came over to collect one of the trays by Mike's table.

The fiendish master appeared besides them as if he might have been waiting behind a black curtain made invisible by the dark. Once again he laughed, more ghoulishly than ever. "You see what it means to underestimate me? To imagine that your feeble perception of this world could ever permit you to peer into the obscure recesses of my designs? You shall serve me or watch this dainty dish ripped open."

Mike shuddered as if he were bleeding to death. This Jolly Roger, in spite of being wracked by insanity that would leave most men moaning on the floor of a padded room, had the planning of a master strategist. He had set a trap for him where he had least expected it, and now Mike was his to do with as he would. He watched Dog Vomit tremble. What a trap, how could they have known? Then the tragic truth became clear. She was one of theirs. It had to be that way. He'd never had any luck in either war or love. But at least he knew and, feeling emboldened by the fact that he had seen through one of Jolly's tricks, it was now his turn to laugh. "Quite frankly she's one of the best you've got. Almost fooled me completely. But if you want to slice her up go ahead."

Jolly let out what might have been a light hearted chuckle but was converted into raucous noise by the voice distorter. "That's exactly what we need. People who are ready to watch their dreams burn and crumble." He then raised his hand in a silent command to red Igor and purple Igor, and they detached Dog Vomit who then jogged spritely to Mike's side.

"I hope you understand," she whispered intimately, "I do like you a lot but I belong to the master." She then turned and skipped into the darkness.

The merriment of "The Master" could not be contained. He shook with electronically modified laughter until he started to cough and the coughs came out like the words of a consonant free language. "Zrt, chrt, fkm, drz, blk, vzk," he went, every distorted syllable another humiliating lash across the back of Mike's already well flayed self-esteem. When he had recovered from his self-induced fit of hilarity, he addressed Mike anew in a harsher tone.

"So you tried to get inside our organization? You should have known that nobody gets inside us. We get inside of them. Now you're going to have to pay a price for your lack of reverence. We shall make a weapon of you and sling you back at the heart of those you've been hired to protect."

Jolly Roger signaled his servants by twirling a finger in the air. They walked towards what appeared to be the recesses of the hangar, but was revealed to be a blackened wall as they approached it with small flashlights in their hands. They then took a hold of it and rolled it away as though it were a soundstage backdrop. Mike guessed that they must be in some abandoned movie studio. Perhaps they had rented the space under the pretext of making a low-budget flick. Mike began figuring the odds of his being rescued. Some maintenance man or union representative might stumble upon these curious, clandestine activities.

He was imagining himself freed when his calculations were abruptly interrupted by the perplexing vision of what lay behind the wheeled barrier. Under lighting slightly more intense than that over the table he was bound to stood dozens of peculiar machines; metal frameworks glinting malevolently in the dark. These structures conformed to the size and shape of a human body, and Mike feared they might be some exotic instruments of torture, some sort of high-tech iron maidens.

Like commonplace furniture movers, the Igors loaded one of the apparatus onto a pallet truck and wheeled it over to Mike. It's queer and horrific appearance caused him to be so fixated upon it as it drew near, that he took no notice of the simultaneous stealthy approach of Jolly, nor of the rotation of the table back to horizontal. Until, with a start, he discovered himself lying with the fearsome contraption on one side and his cruel captor on the other.

This time the sadistic seer neglected to laugh and merely let out a shrill sigh. "Before I introduce you to our titanium friend here, I'd like you to benefit more directly from some of the research that my many minions concoct." Jolly then paused dramatically so the image of laboratories full of mad scientists all at his service could imprint itself upon Mike's imagination. "Do you like horror films? I'm sure you've guessed that I'm a big fan. And do you know what my favorite monster is?" Mike shook his head feebly. "Come on, take a stab at it."

"Vampires? You'd make a good Dracula."

"Vampires? No, no they've too much romantic potential and romance is really not my thing. Want to pick again? If you're right you'll get a prize. How about smoking some of that good weed and getting naked with Dog Vomit?"

Mike glared at the mask hovering over him. "You'd definitely make a good pimp."

"A pimp? Now that's an idea. Maybe I've missed my calling, but you're in the wrong category. We're talking about horror film characters."

"You'd make a good side show freak."

"You think so? One of those painfully crippled and contorted wonders that circus goers used to gawk at with awe and revulsion?" Jolly picked up a wicked looking surgical implement. "Freaks and geeks have always fascinated me, and as long as you're tied down here I might just make one of my very own." Jolly waved the blade back and forth a bit before putting it away. "Luckily for your sake, I've something else in mind. Which brings me back to my favorite monster, the zombie."

"Why don't you kill yourself? Maybe you'll come back as one."

"That's an interesting suggestion, but I'm talking about real zombies, like the ones that used to work in the sugar cane fields of Haiti. Did you know that they were real? They were victims of a sort of paralytic potion. I've been able to get a hold of some and I've been dying to try it out."

Jolly reached over to the instrument table and picked up a syringe and a vial. He prepared an injection and stuck the needle in Mike's arm. "You sick shit," Mike moaned as a wooziness filled him. Soon his entire body felt numb. He tried to look about him but his paralyzed eyes with unblinking lids were locked upon the ceiling. He discovered that he couldn't move his fingers or toes. He wanted to curse the man that had done this to him but found that he was speechless as well.

Mike heard a clanking sound close to him and imagined that something was being prepared, something for him, something bad. Then the sound stopped and the table pivoted back to vertical. The machine was set up facing him as if it were a partner waiting for him to step forward and dance with it. The Igors detached Mike and strapped him into the metallic skeleton, which held him so firmly that it was if it had become a part of him. He heard a muted humming and saw his hand come into view in front of his face. He hadn't tried to raise his hand and couldn't have even if he had wanted to. He realized that the thing which he was attached to must be some sort of sophisticated robot.

It hummed again and turned Mike about so that he was facing Jolly Roger who was now holding a control box with several joy sticks. "Now you truly belong to me and I can make you do as I will." His perverse imprisoner then fiddled with the joysticks and Mike spun around again and then began marching into the darkness. After about twenty paces he halted and, about facing, goose stepped back.

"This thing is really fun but it's not very subtle. If we refined it a bit we could have you walk right up to whoever we wanted and do whatever we wanted to them. That would be amusing. We could have you fondle somebody." Jolly used control box to make Mike reach out and caress a pair of imaginary breasts. "Or I could make you tear somebody's face off," Jolly turned a nob and Mike found himself making deadly looking claw handed swipes in the air in front of him.

The machine forced Mike to thrash about so frantically that it was almost as if the will to do so was coming from within him and it was merely enabling him to express some murderous rage that he had been holding back. After buffeting him about to the point where the shadows around him were spinning, the motorized framework suddenly froze as if all its joints had been welded solid. When his eyes were once again able to focus he saw Jolly before him, the control box gone from his hands. In its place was a belt bearing a dozen cigarette pack size boxes.

The master held it up for the poor slave's appreciation as if their roles had become inversed and he was now presenting him with some conciliatory offering. Mike examined it as well as his rigidified view permitted. It might be an ammo belt but the box shapes weren't pouches. Then he remarked a larger black box where the buckle would normally be and wires running from it to the other boxes. The awful truth forced itself upon his cringing mind; Jolly was planning to use him as a suicide bomber.

The bloodthirsty madman approached and strung the belt around Mike's waist. "A perfect fit," he quipped and then stood back to appreciate it. He then reached behind himself and brought forth the control box once again. He set Mike to walking around in a tight circle. "It doesn't sag at all when you move, perfect. If it wasn't for the noise and the stiffness of the gait, I could have you walk up on somebody, or a group of somebodies, and blow them all to pieces."

He turned to the Igors. "I thought I told you to get these things ready!" The pair merely shrugged and hung their heads like scolded children. "I'll have to find another use for them. Detach him and put him back." As soon as Mike was strapped down on the table the trio disappeared without a word, leaving him there as if he were just another gadget.

THIRTY THREE

After a few hours the paralysis wore off and Mike could thankfully blink his burning eyes. After several more hours another hooded shape came near, this one all in grey. Mike caught sight of a metal oval in its hands and feared a new round of abuse until he realized to his relief it was a bedpan. The mute figure refused to undo the straps and so, though Mike was saved the indignity of soiling himself, he had to endure that of having his pants pulled down by someone made-up as a cheap horror movie extra. He was then spoon fed a tasteless sort of mush and made to sip some water from a bottle.

He calculated that he had spent a day or so tied to the table, the monotony interrupted by nothing other than the occasional appearance of the grey ghoul to take care of his needs, when Jolly decided to put in another appearance. Mike didn't see him

259

come. He simply heard a buzzing sigh beside him and turning with a start spotted the hideous figure hovering in the shadows. "Didn't mean to startle you. Just thought you might want to be kept up to date on things. We haven't done a thing since you fell into our claws, but the world outside seems to be going crazy."

Jolly pivoted Mike's bed to vertical and then snapped his fingers. The purple and crimson Igors rolled a television out of the shadows. They passed him the remote control and he switched it on. A square of bright color lit up amidst the gloom like a window to another world. The familiar face of a female television journalist filled half the screen. Behind her rose the gleaming glass facade of police headquarters. "This is Jane Werk of LAV News coming to you live. Authorities have just released the details of an incredible development in the celebrity stalkers case. In a highly unusual series of events, an LAPD detective was kidnapped with the apparent intention of extracting information from him. Apparently a powerful individual or group with connections to both the film industry and organized crime hired the kidnappers."

The news program cut to three burly men being led on a perp walk, arching their thick necks into painful looking contortions to escape the glare of the cameras. Their efforts were all in vain; their mug shots were displayed on the screen as the journalist continued her exposé. "John Sims, Brian Mole, and Jack Sprat have all been arrested numerous times on suspicion of being involved in high-profile assassinations."

The icy stares of the three alleged hit men were allowed several seconds of screen time before the reassuring features of the reporter came back on. "The target of their crime was a veteran police detective, Mark Ruh." The photo of a younger, uniformed Ruh with a cocksure smile was presented for the viewer's appreciation before Miss Werk came back on. "Detective Ruh was reported missing early yesterday morning. An anonymous tip led investigators to an abandoned garage in Venice Beach." The said garage was then shown surrounded by SWAT. "After the building was secured the detective was released and the men, that the police say kidnapped him, were taken into custody."

While the tele-journalist narrated Ruh was shown being wheeled on a gurney from an ambulance into a hospital, a cordon of uniformed police holding back a surging mass of cameramen. "Authorities say that Detective Ruh was subject to torture by his captors. The principle means used appears to have been waterboarding. We have obtained video of these torture sessions, apparently recorded by the torturers themselves. We advise sensitive viewers to abstain from watching due to its graphic nature."

Three men in ski masks standing over a man tied to a chair with a sack over his head were shown. One of the standing men picked up a bucket and began to pour water over the fabric of the sack, while the other held it tight to their victim's face.

The bound man soon began to thrash and sputter. Only when he had collapsed into a senseless state was the sack removed to reveal him to be Detective Ruh.

The man that had held the sack slapped him awake. "Who do you take orders from? Who is behind all of this?"

Ruh gasped for breath. "I take orders from the captain of my division. Who is behind what?"

"Don't act like you don't know what we are talking about. We know you're working with the celebrity killers, and you're going to tell us everything you know about them."

"I only know what I've found out in the course of our investigation, which isn't much. Whoever's in charge of it all knows how to insulate himself."

"So, you're going keep acting like you're not a part of it? You're going to breathe water till you give us some names."

As his interrogator began to place the sack over his head again Ruh desperately proclaimed his innocence. "But I don't know nothing! You've got the wrong person!"

Ruh's protests were cut off as the drowning began again. He began rocking frantically back and forth trying to turn the chair over and escape, but it was bolted to the floor. After he had passed out again, he was once more roughly brought around. The head of the brutalized man flopped weakly from side to side like a dying fish before hanging limply down, his chin touching his chest. "You can keep on until you kill me. I've nothing to do with any of these crimes."

For a third time he torturers took hold of the head of the man who no longer offered any resistance. The images of further abuse were cut out in order to jump to a scene that, from the time displayed in the upper right hand corner, took place some forty minutes later. Ruh was sagging against the ropes that held him to the chair, as pale as a corpse. The kidnappers smoked cigarettes while studying him as if he were a complicated piece of stone or wood, and they were craftsmen hired to work him into a certain shape.

Suddenly SWAT burst into the garage. One team threw the casually smoking trio to the ground with such force that their cigarettes arced through the air, while another cut their captive free and laid him out on the floor. The only evidence of life he displayed was his gasping mouth.

The broadcast then cut to a revived Ruh lying in a hospital bed ready to give a statement to the microphones surrounding him. "I've no idea whatsoever why these sick criminals picked me. There is no evidence at all that I've any connection with the stalkers. Moreover, I've already had a trial, a trial by waterboarding."

Jolly switched off the television and the Igors rolled it back to whence it had come. Mike thought that he could just make out a twinkle of evil delight in the eyes behind the mask. The perverted genius stood gloating for a while before adding his own commentary.

"So what did you think? The world's just getting crazier and crazier ain't it?"

"Well it has a way to go before it catches up with you."

"Oh, so you are learning. That's what I showed you this reportage for. So you can understand just how it's all going to breakdown, leaving me in charge."

"You think that by killing celebrities you're going to become master of the world? They're going to have to make up a whole new psychiatric classification in order to diagnose you."

"So, you've had some experience with being evaluated by psychiatric professionals. I thought as much."

"Everybody in the service is subject to an evaluation."

"Yes of course, but I think that in your case they ended up taking things a bit further. I can almost guess what conclusion they came to. Or might I say conclusions. I'm almost certain there were several conflicting ones. If you went to regular doctor and he said you had lung cancer and then you went to another and he said you had chronic bronchitis then you'd say there was something seriously wrong with their profession. But head doctors, you can go to a dozen and have as many diagnoses and hardly anyone one faults them for their inconsistency."

"So what the fuck does it matter? I'm nobody. You're the one who wants the world to take him seriously. There must be several teams of psychiatrists attached to various law enforcement agencies who are putting together profiles of you, and I'm pretty sure that you wouldn't find any of them complementary."

"But you have to understand that being complemented isn't really my goal. Hatred and fear are what I'm aiming at, at least in the beginning. Hatred and fear that will ultimately morph into groveling awe, perhaps even deification."

"Wow, that's sure some agenda you've got there pal. But I don't see why you need little old me in your plot for world domination. Like I said I'm nobody."

"But that's why you're so essential. You're just an ordinary person who's happened to find himself in the epicenter of a conflict from which all the tomorrows shall emerge. You're the one they'll all be talking about."

"Like I said before, 'wow', and thanks but no thanks. You've got so many loons and goons ready to do whatever you say. I don't really know why you need me."

"You shall see. You shall understand. You will come to accept this as your destiny."

"I don't want a destiny. I just want a quiet life. Is that too much to ask?"

"In your case, yes. You have been chosen, and I don't take no for an answer."

Mike lay looking up at the shadows above him wracking his brain for a comeback. Perhaps something witty was the answer. A quip that would amuse the madman in whose mercy he found himself and convince him that he would be best used as simple comic relief instead the lead player in this dark and twisted drama. He was on the point of formulating a whimsical phrase that was certain to make them all break out with uproarious laughter when he noticed that they had vanished. He lay there for hours trying to conserve in his mind the words that he hoped would free him from whatever dire fate they held in store for him. But after hours of being assailed by haunting memories and dread foreboding, it eroded like a chalk cliff lashed by centuries of surging waves.

And as if they themselves had been the wind driving those waves, Jolly and the two Igors appeared again just as the last grains of Mike's witticism were washed away. In the sickly shimmering light Mike could make out a human figure attached to a dolly that the purple Igor was wheeling towards him. Mike wondered whether it was some new device or perhaps another captive. But when they came to a stop before him Mike realized to his revulsion that it was a human corpse.

THIRTY FOUR

Jolly slapped the cadaver on the shoulder congenially and its mouth popped wide open as if it might inhale itself back to life with a deep inspiration of the fetid air. Jolly cocked his head toward the body's pallid features. "Were you about to say something? We're dying to hear it." After allowing himself a boorish laugh at his own poor attempt at humor, he pushed the dolly so close to Mike that the odor of decay and embalming fluid filled his nostrils.

"Do you recognize our new playmate here?"

Mike wondered whether the fiends had taken to murdering his friends and acquaintances in an effort to further break his will, but then he remembered that he didn't really know anyone, not anymore. But perhaps they had hunted down some childhood companion and brought back his remains as a trophy. He studied the face closely for any resemblance to a barely remembered classmate. For some reason the gaping mouth recalled the image of someone, someone singing. Was this some former choirboy brought before him to silently chant the praises of a new lord, Jolly Roger? But Mike had never sung in any church. He had never even sung in foreign bars filled with drunken servicemen braying songs from home. So where had he seen this face singing?

Suddenly, a certain high frequency sputtering in the lights above lit things up with a glow similar to that of a TV screen and reminded Mike of where he'd seen the now grisly face, delicately made up and cheerfully lip syncing, a music video. That was it. Though Mike couldn't quite put a name to the face, the story behind it had so saturated the media that even the most isolated individuals had been force fed the tragic tale.

He had been a teenaged pop-star whose forlorn beauty and mournful crooning of angst filled lyrics had millions of adolescent girls staring at giant posters of him on their walls as they explored their young bodies and obsessed upon each word that passed his lips as if it were a message destined for them alone. Mike remembered thinking that maybe the world would be a better place if the teen idol died an ugly death and then feeling a tiny prick of guilt when he drowned in his own vomit after ingesting a hefty dose of prescription and non-prescription drugs and washing it down with a bottle of vodka. Whether it had been an overdose or a suicide had never been determined. But now, seeing the body in the hands of the monsters responsible for so many deaths, Mike speculated that he had been the victim of a well disguised murder.

Jolly stuck his head forward and shook it so the mask rattled like something suddenly come to life. "We need you to be somebody. Somebody that everybody is talking about." He then paused and stepping behind the corpse placed his rubber gloved hands upon its shoulders as if it were the living body of a beloved son. "This boy here and I have gotten to know each other." He gripped the shoulders squeezing a bit of the putrefied liquid out of them and leaving a lightened impression of his hands. "I've watched the changes he has gone through since his death. Through these changes he expressed something to me, something poignant, a deep desire. After several days of watching him decay I realized what he wanted, to perform once more, to give one final ovation to his public."

As Jolly was finishing talking the red Igor rolled one of the robotic metal frames up beside the dead pop star. "So what are you going to do? Have him dance around naked? I don't think you're going to get him to sing."

"No, I'm going to have him perform with you."

"Sorry to disappoint you but I'm not much of an entertainer."

"Don't worry you'll do alright."

"What kind of number are we going to do?"

"Take a look at his cock."

269

"No thanks. I'm not really interested."

"Look at it," Jolly commanded.

Mike felt compelled to look at the body's member. It was surprisingly large for someone with such a childish face and slight build. To his disgust Jolly began kneading the scrotum.

Mike wanted to look away but couldn't, "Okay, you're the most perverted motherfucker in the world. Do you want a special prize?"

"Look closer and you'll see that I'm only getting it ready for you."

Mike glanced back at the cadaverous genitalia and then turned towards the eyes behind the mask, searching desperately for a trace of humanity in their demonic glare. "Getting it ready for me?"

"Yes, look upon it once again!"

The deceased's organ had grown larger and more erect. "What are you doing?"

Jolly's evil laugh crackled through the voice distorter, "Maybe this boy didn't have enough love in his life. So we're going to give him one last chance and it seems like you are just his type. We've equipped him with an inflatable penile implant especially for this occasion."

The monstrosity and repulsion of what they had in plan for him made Mike's whole body shiver as if he had been thrown into an icy sea. A bright light was shone upon him and he could barely make out through the glare that the purple Igor was pointing a camera at him. "But you can't do this. It's inhuman."

"That's right, it's the next step. Humanity's dead and gone and we're leaving it far behind. We're going to put you and lover boy here up on the internet doing the act. Then the whole world will be ready for whatever comes next."

As Mike watched in dread the red Igor attached the corpse to the robotic frame. He then did something to the table Mike was on so the bottom split in two. This enabled him to spread Mike's legs apart. Jolly then slipped a portable control panel out from under his shroud and used the joysticks to walk the remote controlled cadaver up between Mike's legs. As the penis of the recently departed teen idol entered him Mike felt as if some essential part of him was being torn out.

Jolly jerked the joystick back and forth inducing an arrhythmic thrusting of the cadaver's pelvis. He hunched over the control panel, craning his neck toward the object of his attentions like a child crouched before a television screen playing a new video game. The purple and red Igors adjusted the lights and the cameras to record every revolting second of the macabre violation. They even panned from the body's face to that of Mike so that the future audience would be assured of the identities of the two.

Within the three arduous minutes of the depraved video Mike was completely transformed. He was like a steer that the slaughterhouse had made a side of beef of. The camera and body were rolled away leaving Mike alone with Jolly.

The pitiless pervert ran his glove across the body of Mike as if he were taking possession of it as his personal property. "So what do you have to say for yourself now?"

Mike lay prostrate in numb silence.

"I told you we would make you into what we wanted and now it's done. The whole world will now be a witness to your debasement, and you will live the rest of your life in the shadow of it. Anything you do, no matter how horrible, can be explained and justified as a reaction to the brutalization you've endured. And when you kill for us, and you will kill for us, you will be seen as a willing accomplice."

With his eyes shut and lips barely parted Mike muttered like someone deep in a dream, "You've killed me, so it doesn't matter, as long as one day I get the chance of getting a shot at you."

Jolly hesitated a few seconds before responding, not long, but long enough to reveal that the threat had been cause for some reflection. "As you died today, I died some while ago. Soon you will understand." The degenerate creature then slipped away, leaving Mike alone to contemplate the abomination that had been enacted upon him.

Mike had been lying on the table reliving the monstrosity he had experienced for several achingly long hours when Jolly and the Igors came back. Jolly rubbed his gloves together eagerly. "Do you know what day today is?"

"I don't care, unless it's the day you die a painful death."

"Ha, ha, good to see you have some spirit left. But no sorry, my demise isn't on the schedule. Today is the day of the Academy Awards, and I feel like a child on Christmas morning."

"You're kind of like a child all the time, a very sick and twisted child who never should have been born."

Jolly bent his neck and brought his hand up to his chin in what might have been a contemplative gesture, if such a monster could be considered to contemplate upon things in anyway like a normal human. "Never have been born, now that's the truth! But how many of us should never have been born, and most of those never once even considering the clumsy and senseless accident of their birth. And they go on with their futile lives, serving those of more well-conceived origins. But I have made from shabby happenstance a glorious destiny, in which those that would toy with me have become in their turn my playthings."

"Wow, that's some speech; do you just improvise this stuff or do you spend hours making it up?"

"I will always have the right word at the right moment. Whether I write or speak it."

"I've just thought of something that, though I might struggle a bit to put it into words, needs desperately to be said."

"Go ahead, say whatever you like."

"Hollywood is full of over inflated egos but none of them can match your pure megalomania. They have all sorts of artistic and social pretensions but if they're really questioned long and hard enough they'll admit that what they're doing is just entertainment."

"Just entertainment? But all of it is entertainment, from the first gasping breath to the last. When it stops being entertaining people usually kill themselves. I will be remembered as the greatest entertainer ever. The one who made all their multi-million dollar extravaganzas look like cheap puppet shows."

"Goddamn, that's some super-duper plan you've got there but why not just let me off the ride. I think I'd do better as a spectator."

"You will be both actor and spectator. I've gotten it all ready for you."

The red and purple Igors stepped forward, the red one bearing an explosive belt in his hands. The red Igor pulled away the sheet covering Mike and lifted his midsection, as the other one attached the deadly girdle to his waist. An ultimate sentiment of helplessness filled Mike. He was now as firmly in their grasp as a new born kitten between the palms of a cruel, animal torturing child who might well grow up to be a serial killer.

The purple Igor then put a Bluetooth in Mike's ear and stepped back to let Jolly stand over Mike. The hi-tech terrorist held another control panel in his hands, this one consisting of only a small video screen and a large red button. He turned the screen towards his prisoner's face and Mike could see displayed upon it an endless series of images of himself upon the bed, like the effect made when two mirrors are set facing each other.

Mike was striving to interpret the implications of the picture on the screen when Jolly volunteered to clarify the situation. "As you are well aware we've got all kinds of special gadgets. This Bluetooth you're wearing is one of them. Not only does it allow us to communicate but also comes equipped with a miniature camera that transmits video to this panel."

Mike moved his head around a bit and saw that the screen displayed a wobbling shot of the cobwebbed rafters above him. Jolly then let the control panel hang on his chest from a strap around his neck so that it was still facing Mike while leaving his hands free. He took a firm hold of Mike's head. "Now you shall obey us." He forced Mike to nod his head and then gave a little laugh that the scrambler translated into a sound like the sputtering of a broken machine.

Looking at the video image of himself Mike was struck dumb by the full weight of his helplessness. These lunatics would use him as a tool of their deranged crusade and then throw him away like a worn out appliance. He had no more chance of escape than a hostage in a Jihadist video about to be decapitated.

Jolly instantly sensed the vulnerability of his captive. The mouth of his mask curved upward with what might have been a wickedly broad smile on the face behind it. "Perhaps we will let you live. In fact I think it will be for the best. Follow my orders and you might have some time left."

"I know you'll kill me no matter what I do. You like killing people."

"Oh, you got it all wrong. I don't so much like killing people, it's just a necessary part of my project. Everybody's got to have a project. Without one life's a waste. Now time's a wasting, you've got to get a move on."

Jolly stepped back clutching the control panel. "We're going to let you free now. Don't get aggressive or you'll be blown in half. The explosives are set to explode inward without harming those around you. But if I push this button they'll need two separate body bags for you."

The red Igor undid the table's straps and made Mike sit up. The purple Igor brought over a tray with a basin of hot water, soap, a washcloth, and a comb. The accumulated grime on Mike's face was quickly wiped away and his hair put in place. The purple Igor then whipped out a straight razor, not to slice Mike's throat, but to skillfully shave his face as if he might once have been a barber.

The purple Igor then brought out a box that contained Mike's uniform. "Dog Vomit stole the key of your apartment and made a copy."

Mike was stunned by the depth and calculation of her treachery. "How could she do that?"

"She's got her ways that girl. Anyway, you're going to get dressed up and go straight to the Academy Awards. Everyone will be so surprised to see you they won't ask any questions. You'll be a kind of hero so you can get right out in front, where the cameras can get a good shot of you. When my favorite stars start up the red carpet I'll say go and you'll jump out and open fire."

"Yeah, sounds like your sick idea of fun. How do I know that you won't just blow me up after I gun down some people?"

"Can't you have a little trust? Anyway, that would be pointless. We want you alive to witness our greatness to the world."

"Talk like that doesn't reassure me much."

"Well you can be goddamn certain of one thing. We will blow you up if you don't follow my instructions. Not only do we have that Bluetooth camera but we've also got live feeds from all the major networks."

"How'd you get that?"

"Maybe we hacked their signal. Maybe we've got people working for them. But anyway you're never going to know so do what you're told."

As if inspired by an obscure god who for vague reasons wished to protect him, a plan began to form in Mike's woozy head. "We're supposed to be wearing different uniforms for the Academy Awards. I'll have to pick up a dress uniform and my work ID at my boss's place."

"That's fine, we'll drop you off near there."

Mike was then handcuffed and a suffocating, blinding sack was fastened over his head. Firm hands guided him down a long echoing concrete floor before emerging into sunlight that, though he couldn't see it, made its heat felt through the stifling fabric. He was then thrust into a van that for an hour or so went on a ride filled with abundant twists and turns, obviously meant to disorient him.

Eventually, the handcuffs were removed and he was forced out of the van with strict orders not to remove the hood before counting to thirty. As he stood there sightless on the sidewalk he could feel people moving past him. They muttered what might be curses under their breath, annoyed with the hooded figure blocking their way but too wary of what the hidden face might hold to insult him out loud.

THIRTY FIVE

Mike finally pulled off the hood and then spent a minute or so squinting before his eyes adjusted to the light. He didn't recognize where he was and so he glanced at the skyline to find a landmark. Everything was obscured by a pinkish orange haze. Its color was almost that of the skin of a heavily made up starlet in a cheap porno movie. The excessive smog was undoubtedly due to the millions pouring into the LA basin for the Academy Awards. Each one of them unknowingly participating in the event by discharging millions of cubic yards of poisonous gas that would form a tangerine pall hanging over the ceremonies.

Passersby refused to stop and give him directions, taking him for a homeless mental case or drug addled beggar. Some even crossed the street a block away from him. He was on the point of trekking off in just any direction when Jolly came over the Bluetooth. "Go two blocks east and then turn right."

"How do I know where east is?"

"Look for where the smog is thickest."

Scanning the horizon Mike noticed that before him lay a patch of dark brown sky like that that a forest fire might make. He strode off in that direction and soon found himself in front of the converted storage facility where Moses lived. He let himself in and rode up to Moses' loft. While putting on the uniform he pulled the shirt half on so that it covered the Bluetooth. He then hastily went to the gun locker and began loading his revolver with blanks.

Jolly began shouting at him, "Don't cover up the camera. What are you trying to pull?"

"Nothing, nothing at all. The collar is kind of tight, and I'm having trouble getting it on."

"Pull it over quick, I don't care if you have to tear it."

Mike let the Bluetooth fall to the floor and the hysterical anger in Jolly's voice hissed through the scrambler. "Put it back on, right now, I'll blow you to pieces."

Fumbling to fill all the chambers with blanks Mike stalled for time. "If I tear it they might notice and not let me in."

"Fucking get it on fast, I want a clear shot of everything you do."

Mike finished loading the revolver and, snapping the cylinder back in place, stuck it in his holster. He then pulled the shirt down and straightened out the Bluetooth. "You see. Everything's just where it's supposed to be."

"Get yourself to the show now!"

"I'm on my way."

Mike ran to the metro and got on a train to the Hollywood and Highland station. He pushed his way up through the pack of bodies jamming the stairs. He then swam through the crowd to a security checkpoint manned by both the LAPD and two security guards for Hollywood Detectives. They instantly recognized him and waved him through as though he were some essential participant. Everyone stood back and stared at him as though he were some captive long given up for dead now miraculously walking amongst them.

Unchallenged, he took a privileged post behind the velvet rope. Limousines began unloading tuxedo and night gown clad bodies with famous faces. These posed in several directions to give sufficient photo ops to all the paparazzi present. Afterwards they passed within arm's length of Mike.

As if he possessed some shark like sense of the presence of his prey, Jolly came on the Bluetooth. "They could all make good targets, but there are some special ones I'm waiting for, keep ready."

Mike thought about what would happen when he opened fire. Pandemonium would doubtlessly erupt. The essential question for him was whether he would get killed in the midst of it. He would have to empty the revolver in the direction of the stars on the steps to convince Jolly that he was making a sincere attempt on their lives and then throw himself on the ground before the police opened fire on him. Hopefully, after taking him prisoner, they would be able to disarm the explosive belt before its crazed controller decided to set it off.

There was a pause in the flow of esteemed personalities up the steps before an exceptionally long, gleaming white Lincoln Continental limo glided up. From it emerged John Stain, a former romantic comedy star who had received a deluge of praise for his portrayal of the transsexual leader of a white supremacist terrorist group. His co-stars streamed out of the stately vehicle after him. They were all carefully chosen ex-head-liners who had made strategically brilliant come-backs by portraying vicious, violent, and perverse white trash with eerie realism.

For some reason they gathered for a group photo a few yards from where Mike was standing. Perhaps they wanted him, the most notorious white trash of the hour, in the shot. Jolly's voice roared over the Bluetooth, "Now, now, go, go, shoot them or I'll blow you apart."

Mike stepped over the barrier towards the cast of the film favored for a half dozen of the evening's awards. None of them seemed surprised; they even had what might have been welcoming smiles on their faces. When he had gotten close enough to almost kiss the leading man he pulled the .32 Colt out and thrust it towards him in a punching motion almost identical to that of Jack Ruby's famous gest and something, perhaps a thespian instinct, made his target crumple like Oswald as Mike fired.

Mike began emptying the revolver towards the rest of the players of the exploitation film with pretentions. Time slowed down and space deformed. He fired the blanks at one performer after another and they all reacted even more hysterically than if they actually been shot. In spite of himself Mike was feeling a strange sort of power. The realization that he regretted not having a more powerful gun with a larger capacity magazine and real bullets shocked him, but it couldn't stop the elation that was coursing through his veins.

He didn't remember how he found himself on his stomach, his arm painfully twisted behind his back and the weight of several heavy bodies' knees crushing him. When he was cuffed a pair of hands slid over him until they found the belt at his waist. "This guy is rigged to blow," a panicked voice shouted.

All but one of the knees released Mike and the voice commanded in a calmer tone, "Don't make a move if you want to live." He heard a knife snap open and felt a twinge of pain as the blade nicked him while slicing through the belt. The explosive girdle was pulled off of him and he was put back up on his feet and duck walked towards a squad car.

They were about to bundle him inside when Detective Ruh appeared. "Let me talk to this one." He stated authoritatively and leaned Mike back against the door. "What was this about?"

"They made me do it. Their leader said he'd blow me up if I didn't."

"So you were ready to kill all these people to save yourself?"

"I tricked them, I put blanks in the gun."

"Blanks, huh. How'd you do that?"

Mike suddenly remembered the suspicion that Ruh had been under. On whose behalf might he be questioning him now? Instead of answering Mike studied his face for any poker tells that might reveal the true game of this potential adversary.

Ruh didn't appreciate Mike's examination much. "You better realize that I'm about the only person on your side there is. And that I'm only on your side because detective Stave insisted upon it."

"Detective Stave?" Mike weighed the significance of her support for a while as he stared towards the west. One of the rare fogs that the ocean breezes manage to push inland was hanging over LA, giving it the appearance of a more idyllic town. Out of this fog rose a droning hubbub, as if some event even more important than the awards was starting.

Ruh shook Mike to get his attention. "Do you know what that is?"

"Whatever it is, it's something very bad."

Ruh spied a TV production van about twenty yards away, and he dragged Mike over to it. After hammering on the door until it slid open, he climbed in pulling Mike after him. The occupants were on the point of pushing them back out when Ruh barked at them. "I'm with the LAPD show me what's going on."

Wordlessly a techie pointed towards a screen. On it a hoard of zombies was advancing down

Hollywood Boulevard. A closer shot revealed that their decayed features had been carefully made up to resemble as closely as possible their living appearance. Mike could make out Clark Gable, Marilyn Monroe and Elizabeth Taylor amongst other famous faces. Jolly must have attached the stolen celebrity bodies to the robotic frames and set them off like windup toys towards the Dolby Theater.

On the screen a fashionably dressed young couple, giggling and pointing, approached the corpse of WC Fields as it wobbled along. When they got close it exploded, disintegrating the pair of them.

"What the fuck!" Ruh exclaimed, "Haven't these bastards done enough. What the hell will stop them?"

"I can stop them," Mike interjected.

"Yeah, how is that?"

"It's too complicated to explain. Let me loose and I'll take care of them."

"How do I know you won't just escape?"

"Escape to where?" Mike nodded at a screen showing an army of celebrity zombies approaching from the east as well. "We're surrounded."

Without another word Ruh undid Mike's cuffs and he ran off towards a line of police who were firing into the advancing ranks of the lurching dead. They were explosively decapitating them with expert marksmanship but to no avail; the headless stars kept advancing. Mike crouched down next to a sergeant wielding an M4 carbine.

"Fire at their bellies," he shouted.

"Who the hell are you?" the sergeant yelled back.

"I was held prisoner by their maker. They've got bombs attached to their waists."

The sergeant let loose a burst at the stomach of the nearest cadaver. It exploded spraying rotten flesh towards them. He then got on his radio to pass on what he'd learned. Soon the streets were still and strewn with carnage, and the gathered crowd, along with the international television audience, gazed upon the scene with a fascinated revulsion akin to that of motorists passing a lurid wreck.

THIRTY SIX

Over the course of an evening of intense interrogation it was decided not to charge Mike with anything, the lives he had saved counting for more than whatever crimes he might be considered to have committed. For the first time in history the Academy Awards were postponed for a week and amazingly Hollywood Detectives were kept on to provide security.

Mike spent most of the week lying in bed, vodka, cannabis indica, and Xanax protecting him from hysteria. When Moses didn't contact him he imagined that he was probably fired and didn't really care. He was mulling over the possibility of checking into a mental hospital for the rest of his life when his cell phone rang. It was Moses. He had a special mission for Mike, and for some reason Mike found himself volunteering.

Moses met him at the door of his loft and led him to a gun cabinet he had never opened before. Inside it was an impressive collection of long guns. Moses pulled out an M 25, an M14 heavy battle rifle adapted for sharp shooting, and passed it to Mike. "Ever handle one of those before?"

"I almost qualified as a sniper. This is my dream weapon."

"Well, you're going to be up in a tower with it tomorrow night, covering the ceremony."

"Don't they have police for that?"

"I've explained to them that I want one of my own people out there too. Someone who's got a special grudge to settle with this cult of crazies."

Mike stroked the stock of the weapon that was ugly and elegant at the same time. "Let's hope they show up. They'll get a very special award."

The next day at three o'clock Moses and Mike met in a barren office on the top floor of the gaudy El Capitan Theater. Moses took the M25 out of an electric guitar case. He then waved Mike over to help him push a desk up to the window. "This will give you a stable firing platform. You can cover the carpet leading up to the show. The roof tops are all taken care of so we're not concerned about a long shot, just some kind of kamikaze wired to explode like you were. You think you can handle that?"

Mike took the weapon and zeroed in on the red carpet that was already lying there waiting to receive the evening's notable guests. "I can handle it. But am I supposed to shoot through the glass? Won't it deflect the bullet a bit?"

"Aim through this pane here." Moses indicated a place in the window a few feet from where Mike was set up.

"Why there?"

Moses reached out and touched it lightly making the surface shiver. "It reflects light the same as the glass but it's a thin plastic film. Shooting through it won't have any effect upon the bullet's trajectory. And no one will know that you're behind it."

"No one? Not even the police?"

"There's no telling what services have been infiltrated. We need you here as a secret ace in the hole."

"Okay, I just hope I get a clear shot at these bastards."

"So do I. I'll leave you here then. Maybe I'll stop by just before the ceremony begins." Moses then set a bag of fast food on the desk. "Here's some grub for you. Stay low and out of sight."

Mike whiled away the hours sitting in the chair lining up different targets from the window, pigeons, tourists, traffic police and such. He was pretty sure that at this range he could take them all out. It gave him a feeling of power knowing that he held their lives in his finger tip while they went about their business blithely unaware. He was so occupied that night fell without him noticing it. He had gulped down his burrito and was wrapping the rifle sling around his arm when Moses stepped soundlessly up behind him, startling him so much that he almost pulled the trigger.

"Everything under control here?"

KILLEBRITY

Mike inspected the boulevard through the telescopic site. A crowd had gathered, jostling each other in eager anticipation. "Nothing to report."

"That's good. The audience will be arriving soon."

"I'm ready."

"You know I didn't tell you the whole truth about my mother."

"Oh, yeah?"

"It's true she did come here to be an actress but she didn't end up as a waitress; she became a whore instead."

Mike felt the way one feels in group therapy just before someone reveals some unpleasant personal experiences that you would rather not know about. "Damn, that must have been harsh."

"Yeah, and then my poor father. He married her to try to save her, but she just kept on whoring. All through school all the kids taunted me. 'Ha, Ha, Moses' mama is a whore.' But me I didn't let it get to me. I knew that I was better than them and one day I'd show it."

A stretch Humvee pulled up in front of the Kodak Theater and a squad of bodyguards and door openers surrounded it like they were part of a military operation. Mike was at a loss of for words. He couldn't even get out something neutral like "oh" or "hmm". Then he heard Moses unsnap his holster and slide out his gun. For some reason the sound made him think of being in a bunk next to someone masturbating and pretending not to hear. Then he felt the barrel pressing against the back of his head.

"What the fuck?" Mike muttered.

"That's right stupid punk! I'm Jolly Roger. I put it together. I used my contacts and my knowledge and when the time came I activated my group. Now you're going to join the party."

"It can't be you. You were with me when I spoke with Jolly."

"Duh, this town is filled with actors. I can always get someone to play my part when I've got other things to do. Just like ancient kings always had doubles to take their place in dangerous times."

"You're insane."

"Insane? Do you know how many psychological tests I've passed? So either I'm sane or psychiatry is meaningless in which case there is no such thing as insane."

"Well there's still such a thing as crazy!"

"Yeah I guess there is but I don't see it as a disease, something pathological. It's more like a selective adaptation. Sometime in the distant past craziness helped man to survive and now in certain of us it still lingers on. Craziness is just like fangs or claws but hidden better."

A silver limo pulled up and a smiling man got out.

"Oh, damn, that's what's his name. I don't like comedy but that guy's funny as hell. Shoot him in the spine so I can watch him twitch around on the ground a bit.

Mike tried to put the rifle down. "I'm not shooting anybody."

"Pick that rifle up or I'll blow your brains out. You work for me. Kill a few people and then you can surrender."

"Surrender?"

"Yeah, surrender to me. I'll take you into custody and everyone will learn that you're the master mind behind the stalking cult."

"But I'll tell everyone it was you."

"Who are they going to believe? A decorated ex-LAPD detective or a combat veteran with psychological troubles?"

Mike jerked his head around at Moses.

"Yep, you've got post-traumatic stress disorder and maybe psychosis. Thought I couldn't get a copy of your file huh? Sounds like a pretty severe case too. You'll probably get off with not guilty by reason of insanity. So your choice; die right now or spend the rest of your life in SHU. People say it's not so bad there if you're on the right medication. You can probably be part of some sort of theater group or something."

Mike looked intensely through the telescopic sight of his rifle at the celebrities filing up the steps to the Kodak Theater. They didn't look at all like real people but more like video characters. It began to seem to him like he was supposed to shoot them.

Then Moses interrupted his morbid reverie. "What the fuck do you want me to do? Give you a count down? Okay, five, four, three, two, one..."

Suddenly a shot rang out. Lisa Stave emerged from the shadows her side arm aimed at Moses who lay on the ground, his body contorting in pain. He lifted his gun to fire back at her and she shot him three more times killing him. The crowd in the street scattered in panic, the celebrities on the carpet cowered in terror, and the police pulled their guns. Lisa re-holstered hers and got out her radio. "It's all clear. I've got the shooter. I'm at the top story of El Capitan and we're coming down."

Mike put the rifle down. "Hey, I wasn't involved."

"I'm a smart girl. I can figure that out. Anyway, since I've saved your life you can at least offer me a drink."

THIRTY SEVEN

Mike parked the flat gray Chevy Nova in front of the bungalow, his unkempt appearance and furtive eyes those of a petty criminal. A haggard and worn looking man got out on the other side.

Mike swiveled his head towards him. "You sure they got what we want?"

"They always got it," the man answered grimly.

They entered the house and a tattooed man with a shot gun frisked them and, after having them open the briefcase to verify its contents, he led them into a trashed out living room. A fat man in a track suit was sitting on the couch. He waved Mike and the man he was with over to two easy chairs sitting across a coffee table from the couch. "You got the money?"

Mike held up the briefcase. "Right here."

"Let me count it."

"Let's see the meth."

The fat man in a track suit took a plastic bag full of white powder and put it on the coffee table. "Try some."

Mike snorted a line and, after staying frozen in place for a long second, he arched his back and rolled his head like some force was stretching him towards the sagging water damaged ceiling.

The lump of blubber on the sofa shook with merriment. "You white trash love that meth. So, my money?"

Mike opened the briefcase and started stacking money on the table. When it had all been unloaded he suddenly opened a false bottom and whipped out a gun. "Police! Don't move!"

The tattooed man with the shotgun rushed into to room. The Mike's seemingly decrepit partner instantly recovered the reflexes of a younger man and, snatching another gun from the briefcase, shot him dead with a rapid double tap, one to the chest and one to the head. Mike took a pair of cuffs from the briefcase and started putting them on the fat man in athletic clothes.

"But you can't be a cop! I saw you sniff that meth!"

"Just a slight feat of prestidigitation!"

"Presta what?"

Mike sat him down on the couch.

"Magic, slight of hand. Like this." Mike showed that his hands were empty and then reached up to the side of the bulging head to pull a nine millimeter bullet from behind its ear.

"But I saw. But I saw."

"You thought you saw."

Just as Mike bent over to heave the fast food fed felon to his feet the director shouted, "Cut! That's a wrap for the day."

Mike turned his eyes towards Lisa Stave who had been sitting in a folding chair observing the scene. As the crew started taking everything down she walked up to Mike. "Pretty convincing."

"Well you're the technical adviser."

"Oh, and do you have some other techniques you'd like some advice on?"

"What about this." Mike gave Lisa a long deep kiss.

"I guess that will work."

And, as the last neurons in Mike's shattered brain shut down due to the damage inflicted by the bullet fired from Moses' gun, he dreamed of finally finding the true love that had eluded him all his sad and lonely life.